INTO THE RISING SUN

INTO THE RISING SUN

Veronica More

The Book Guild Ltd
Sussex, England

First published in Great Britain in 2005 by
The Book Guild Ltd
25 High Street
Lewes, East Sussex
BN7 2LU

Copyright © Veronica More 2005

The right of Veronica More to be identified as the author of this work has been asserted by her in accordance with the Copyright, Designs and Patents Act 1988.

All rights reserved. No part of this publication may be reproduced, transmitted, or stored in a retrieval system, in any form or by any means, without permission in writing from the publisher, nor be otherwise circulated in any form of binding or cover other than that in which it is published and without a similar condition being imposed on the subsequent purchaser.

All characters in this publication are fictitious and any resemblance to real people, alive or dead, is purely coincidental.

Typesetting in Baskerville by
Keyboard Services, Luton, Bedfordshire

Printed in Great Britain by
CPI Bath

A catalogue record for this book is available from
The British Library

ISBN 1 85776 844 2

*In memory of Tom
and for our four children*

The Cove

From where she sits on the arched veranda of her whitewashed villa she can see the jetty clearly. The veranda is a wonderful vantage point and she is aware of most of the day's activity down on the jetty. At this moment of the evening the last of the swimmers are putting on their beach shoes, picking up their towels. Parents collect reluctant children from the water's edge. A handful of teenagers, independent or unmindful of parental admonition, lark about in the now darkening water of a quietly lapping sea.

The villa, which is called Piedras in recognition of the stony ground on which it was built, is situated on a slight rise above a bay that is small enough to be intimate but which falls away almost immediately to the right to form a zigzag coastline dotted with little inlets. The villa's small garden has steps down to a wooden door in the whitewashed wall which encloses it. From the door it is only a few seconds to the water's edge where the beach is pebbles mixed with gritty sand. In the rough weather, wads of seaweed get washed up and then dry out in the intensive summer sunshine into mounds of dry, papery strips. Most swimmers however, use the concrete jetty which juts out from a huddle of what were once fishermen's cottages. Now all the cottages, except one, are owner-occupied by the heirs of those earlier fisherfolk. The façades are unchanged except perhaps for more colourful paint on the shutters but the interiors have been modernised and the roofs bristle with TV aerials. In the winter the cottages are empty, their owners retreating a few kilometres inland to the small town which scrambles up a pear-shaped hill, and from which they may make sporadic appearances on sunny weekends.

Only the cognoscenti swim here. About half a kilometre away, round the headland, sprawl the tourist beaches of fine white sand, overlaid by human bodies and all the paraphernalia people bring to the beach. There, the blue-green water is alive with bobbing heads, plastic toys and lilos, with the occasional intrusion of something more lethal like a wind surfer or a jet ski. Further out, beyond the swimmers, are the water skiers, the pleasure craft and, just now and again, a real fishing boat bound on business not pleasure. Towering over all this are the great concrete hotels and apartment blocks with just here and there, squeezed between them in incongruous juxta-position, a single-storeyed traditional cottage which has somehow escaped the bulldozers. Very little of this spills over into Pebble Cove, as the locals call it. It is more for swimmers than sunbathers. Every now and again a stranger discovers it, adopts it for few days and then is never seen again.

Faith takes her eyes off the jetty as it gradually empties and picks up her book again, which she had laid down open on the white plastic table by her right arm. The slight breeze has ruffled the pages. It is this year's Booker winner. The author is not European and it is a long tale of fact and fantasy which both fascinates and confuses Faith. She has moved her useless left hand into a position where it can act as a sort of prop for the book, so that the whole weight does not rest on her right hand. Her mind has gone blank, she has no memory of where she left off. Turning back several pages, she reads at random until the blank space fills up. She remembers and turns to the page where she stopped reading. Unlike other prisoners, she is not enclosed by bars but she is imprisoned nevertheless.

She had always felt her name to be something of a misnomer. Faith in the conventional religious sense she never possessed. It was not something she had lost, she just never had it. Neither did she feel the need to seek for it. She does have her own brand of faith but that is something different, nothing to do with the established religion into which she was baptised. She was born towards the end of the First World War, at a time when *not* to christen one's children would have been a major statement and not, as perhaps nowadays, mere spiritual laziness or apathy, a fashionable trend, or even just plain forgetfulness.

When her first child was born, Faith deliberated whether or not she should be baptised.

'I can't see what your problem is, darling,' said Morgan, her first husband. 'I'm an atheist and you're agnostic. So to what purpose should we have the child baptised? Social convention?'

Put like that the decision seemed obvious. Later on when Hilary, as their daughter was named, came to confront the nature of existence, the presence or absence of an all-seeing deity, she took matters into her own hands and was baptised and confirmed in her mid-teens.

Faith shifts awkwardly in the wheelchair. With her good hand and active right arm she retrieves the useless left one which has slipped yet again off the arm rest and is dangling down the side of her chair. She brings it up, bends it at the elbow and arranges it across her lap. There is minimal movement in the fingers but no grip and in spite of exercises it does not improve. She stretches out her right leg and flexes it, no paralysis there and it is still tanned from the summer's swimming – before all this happened. She tries moving her left leg and is met as usual by the dull heaviness of no reflex.

She feels a curious detachment from the paralysed side of her body, viewing it objectively as if somehow it does not really belong to her. Just a few days ago, observing it in just such a detached manner, a memory was sparked off from a distant past. It was of an historical novel she had read in her teens, in which there was a nauseating description of a young boy who dragged around with him in the filth of his mediaeval village the putrefying corpse of his Siamese twin to which he was still attached. She had thought with relief – at least I'm not putrefying, not yet anyway.

She looks always for the chink of light in this sombre situation. Depressing though her plight is, she feels for the moment there is reason to be thankful. The shrinking process may have begun, but for the present she is left with her vocal cords, most of her marbles and a right-hand side which still answers to the messages sent to it by her brain. To be able to talk, to communicate, even if groping with increasing frequency now for certain words, is an incomparable bonus.

Hilary comes out on to the terrace through the blue fly curtains from the spacious, coolly tiled living room. She is carrying what looks to be a small, cardboard shoe box. She approaches her mother's chair.

'Are you still warm enough? Or would you like to come in?'

It is mid-September and the summer heat of July and August has continued unabated into the first half of the month. The only concession to approaching autumn is that a certain coolness, fanned by a light breeze, does descend once the sun has disappeared behind the umbrella pine clad hill at the back of the villa.

'It's still quite warm,' Faith replies. 'What's that you've got there?'

She feels she is very lucky to have Hilary. It has been easier for her to obtain leave from her job, to delegate responsibilities and get away promptly than for her younger sister whose job and family are endlessly demanding. Aware of this, Faith tries very hard not to wish Jocelyn were here instead. Hilary is calm, efficient and endlessly patient, and Faith feels twinges of guilt that she should hanker after the scatty warmth of her younger daughter.

'Letters, I think,' replies Hilary. 'You'd best go through them and see if you want to take any with you.'

Faith lets go of her book and it falls open on her lap. She stretches out her right hand to take the box but Hilary does not hand it to her.

'No, mother, it's far too heavy for you to take like that. I just wondered if you would know immediately what letters they are. If you want to go through them I'd best undo the rubber bands and lay them out on the dining room table.'

'Not now, Hilary. I don't feel up to it. I'll do it in the morning.' Faith's voice sounds tetchy.

'All right.' Hilary's tone is accepting. 'But don't forget, time is getting on. There's still a lot to go through.'

Faith laughs inwardly at the unconscious irony of Hilary's remark. Time is indeed getting on, has been getting on, in fact, ever since the moment of birth. Time, our constant companion. Friend or foe? Invisible, untouchable, it has no substance, only deadly significance. As a child Faith was urged not to waste time. As Morgan's wife she valued time. As Morgan's widow time loitered listlessly. And now indeed, as Hilary had just said, time was getting on – a simple euphemism for time running out. Faith knows that in the not very distant future she and Time, as it is known in this world, must part. But of course that was not what Hilary was referring to, she meant that the date of their return to England was getting nearer.

Faith is aware that among the letters in that box are still several from Oliver. Perhaps she should tell Hilary to jettison the lot without her going through them. Did she really want to regurgitate the inevitable failure of her second marriage by reading again Oliver's didactic denial of the truth? He lied with such sincerity that he wholly convinced himself. In retrospect Faith sees that Time for her had been cataplectic during that hideous period. At the memory a tremor creeps up her right side.

'I think I'll come in after all,' she says to Hilary who has turned to go. 'The breeze is cooler this evening.'

'OK. Just let me get rid of this.' Hilary disappears into the house and comes out again without the box. She turns her mother's chair away from the sea view and wheels her inside, Faith stretching out her good arm to part the fly curtains as they pass through.

Faith's stroke happened two months back. She had returned from a fruitful and busy visit to England where she had spent ten days with Hilary and her friend Winnie in their London flat, two weeks in the country with Jocelyn and Mike and the fast growing grandchildren, and shorter visits to friends. She had managed to take in a couple of theatres, a concert and three films. On her return her suitcase had been laden down with the odd hardback and a generous supply of paperbacks to see her through the long hot summer.

Tiredness had dogged her when she returned home to her villa by the sea and she had been glad there were no visitors on the horizon for the first month. Maria had been unwell and Faith had had to manage without any help in the house. As Maria also did the bulk of the shopping this was an additional chore. Faith had given up her car at the beginning of the year, after an accident which left her with a stiff shoulder, but she was now regretting her decision and thinking of remedying it.

Throughout the years that Faith has lived here she has been an assiduous swimmer during the long summer months. Swimming is a pleasure which came to her late in life and for that very reason it has endlessly delighted her. As a child she had been terrified of the water and had never learnt to swim. She still remembers in vivid focus her first contact with the sea.

Mr and Mrs Bailey and their little daughter were spending a summer holiday in Cornwall. Faith's mother sat perched on one low rock while her back rested against another, softened by the small cushion she always carried on outdoor excursions. Her long elegant legs were tucked up under the sweeping cotton skirt which she had arranged in a becoming swirl. A green linen hat, of the same material as her blouse, shaded her face from the sun and cast a shadow on the pages of the Mary Webb novel she was reading. At the water's edge Mr Bailey and his five-year-old daughter were plopping stones into the sea and trying, with little success, to skim some of the flatter ones. Little Faith was dressed in a bright blue bathing dress with puffball legs. striped with white and reaching nearly to her knees. On her head she wore a blue rubber bathing helmet which had a rather unpleasant smell. Quite a vain child, she had tried this outfit on at home and pranced in front of her nursery mirror admiring herself. Her father was clad in a black swimming suit, the legs of which also reached nearly to his knees.

Suddenly he picked Faith up, saying 'And now you're going to learn to swim.' He waded out into the sea and as he plunged and staggered on the slippery stones, a terrified Faith clung round his neck. He waded out until he stood waist deep in the water, then he loosened Faith's arms from around his neck and tossed her into the sea. She let out a scream and landed with a splash.

'Swim, Faith, swim! Use your arms and legs how I showed you,' Mr Bailey shouted encouragingly.

Faith submerged and rose again, flailing her arms and legs. She made a grab for her father's knees and tried to raise herself out of the water. He bent down to disengage her but she seized his hand and clung on with a vicelike grip, screaming, 'Take me out, Daddy! Take me out!'

Mrs Bailey, who could not swim and had no ambition to do so, on hearing all the hullabaloo lowered her book and glanced down the beach. She saw her husband and daughter in the sea together. Harry was there. Harry was in charge, everything was all right. She returned to her reading but soon looked up again as the screaming drew nearer. She saw her husband approach with an hysterical child in his arms. He set her down and Faith rushed to her mother, burrowing her head into the smooth, cotton-covered lap. Hastily Mrs Bailey extracted from a large raffia bag a spotless white towel and wrapped it around Faith.

'What has been going on, Harry?'

'I was trying to teach her to swim.'

'Weren't you perhaps a little bit precipitate, dear?'

'Well my father took me out in a rowing boat and chucked me in the water. That's how I learnt to swim.'

'You were a *boy*, Harry,' his wife said with gentle scorn.

Crestfallen, Mr Bailey turned away and went back to the sea for a swim. He was not a cruel father, nor a brutal man, he just had no imagination.

* * *

Faith could still recall the smell of that rubber bathing helmet. It had been Morgan who had encouraged her to learn to swim. She went to swimming baths and took a few lessons, but she was always a nervous swimmer, unwilling to go out of her depth and doubtful of her capacity to keep afloat. All that changed when she came with Charles to the Mediterranean. From the boat she had no choice but to swim in deep water and she soon learned to trust herself in that buoyant sea.

Throughout the summer Faith usually swam thrice daily. She spent the longest time down on the quay during the course of the morning, going several times into the water and swimming out to the sandy patch which shines luminous green in the dark blue water. She would pass the time of day with the local families whom she saw summer after summer, and would watch their children, of all ages, enjoying themselves. Very early, even as babies, they would be introduced gradually and gently by their parents into the shallow water lapping the shore. In the warm sunshine the water is to them a friendly element. Faith would remember ruefully her own very different initiation. In the evenings she very often swam after everyone else had gone – a brief brisk dip.

But it was the first swim of the day that she treasured most. On some mornings it was spellbinding: the sun, just risen, casting its pale shaft of light along the pearl grey surface of a silken sea; a trembling silence in the landscape with no one about except for perhaps a solitary jogger on the coastal path. Faith would swim along this shaft of light, accompanied sometimes by the two cormorants who often rested motionless on a nearby rock. She swam out to the mouth of the bay where she turned to come back, observing the cottages and her own house bathed in this early light, contrasting sharply with the dark mass of the hill behind them.

On that last morning as she swam out, she thought how pure and hopeful is this first hour after dawn, when all things seem possible, when dreams ride high until they are splintered by the advancing day, so that by nightfall we are grateful to collect any crumbs of the day's achievements. What a way to die, she had thought, swimming endlessly into the rising sun. But not yet. No, no – not yet awhile.

As she neared the jetty she had seen a man in swimming trunks come out of the foreign-owned cottage (none of the locals were early morning swimmers). Presumably he was the new tenant, they seemed to change fortnightly. She felt a stab of annoyance when she saw him, she did not wish to share the sea at this time of the day. As she pulled herself up out of the water she saw he was sitting on the low parapet next to her towel. She greeted him grudgingly in the language of the country and he replied in his own tongue which was German.

It was when she sat down beside him to dry her feet and put on her beach shoes that it happened. As she was bending over she suddenly collapsed in a heap, rolling over on to her left-hand side. She was aware of the man bending over her and attempting to help her to her feet. She tried to say something but nothing came out. The man was a doctor and it did not take him very long to realise what had happened.

By the time the ambulance arrived she was able to speak again but her affected limbs remained obdurate. Maria had been summoned by telephone and she accompanied Faith in the ambulance to the hospital. From there she telephoned Faith's daughter Hilary in London.

Decisions

Hilary has gone out in her hired car to shop at the supermarket. Faith, in her wheelchair, sits up at the dining room table with the letters neatly laid out in front of her. Hilary put them there after breakfast. Around her Maria swishes her damp mop across the tiles.

The sea is turbulent today, no one swims and the temperature has dropped several degrees. During the storm last night dust and leaves have blown in beneath the shutters. Faith feels somewhat chilly as she sits there, reluctant to start on the letters. She asks Maria to fetch her long-sleeved cotton cardigan.

As she watches Maria go into her bedroom she imagines how the villa could have been constructed with just her present situation in mind. There are no stairs. The three bedrooms open off a commodious central area which serves both as a sitting room and dining space. The doors are generous and the wheelchair passes through them with ease. Two of the bedrooms share a communicating bathroom and the large bedroom – Faith's – has its own. For some time now the third bedroom has been in use as a sitting room during the winter months; easily heated and intimate, it gave Faith a cosy protection during bad weather, a protection which was as much psychological as physical. When Jocelyn and Mike visited in the summer she would squeeze the two children into her winter sitting room on fold-up beds.

During the time Faith was in the hospital, being subjected to intensive physiotherapy, her mind had ranged over the possibilities for her future. With understandable, if uncharacteristic, lack of realism she imagined herself coping in Piedras with extra help from Maria.

She had always been quite a controlling sort of person. Jostled and thrown off course as she had been several times in her life, she unfailingly recovered her bearings eventually and mostly by her own efforts. She was slow therefore to appreciate that this time it might be different. It was not until she got home and the hospital staff were no longer there to help her and jolly her along, that she came fully to realise the extent of her disability.

Although she has become skilled in manoeuvring her wheelchair, in making the maximum use of her working limbs and innovative in the way she manipulates her useless arm to be of some help rather than an endless hindrance, frustration rises to the surface and she becomes angry at her impotence. She cannot go to the lavatory unaided. Either Hilary or Maria has to help. This bothers her less than some of the other things. She is not unduly prudish about bodily functions, but the spilt food, mugs or glasses of liquid accidentally dropped or knocked over – that worries her more, and the inability to cope with a newspaper.

After a day or two at home she had begun to perceive the true extent of her loss of control but was unwilling to acknowledge it openly until finally she was obliged to confront the future with a degree of reality.

It was late one night about two weeks after her return from hospital. She was in bed, lying back on her pillows and listening to Haydn's 'Creation' on the radio. She had always loved Haydn's music which she found optimistic and clear-cut – like crystal. She was thinking, as Hilary walked through her open bedroom door, how more than ever his music uplifted her.

Hilary was wearing her silk pyjamas and she sat down

on her mother's bed. The night was balmy and Faith had no more than a sheet over her.

'Are you quite comfy?' Hilary asked.

Faith nodded, keeping her attention on the music. Hilary slapped at a mosquito which was buzzing round her head.

'We'll have to make some plans,' she said. 'Decide what's best to do.'

'Do?' Faith, still tuned in to her listening, felt that she was about to be brought face to face with a problem she would prefer not to admit to.

'Yes. We have to make a plan about your future – we have to decide. As you know I can't stay on here indefinitely.'

'Oh I know, Hilary, and I'm so grateful to you for coming. It's been such a comfort having you with me. But I'll be all right with Maria and we can get some extra help.'

'Mother, you can't stay on here! We have to be practical. You know Maria is nearly as old as you are. She's just not up to looking after you as you need to be looked after. Besides she has her own family. Her husband is not very well and she does quite a bit of grandchild minding as well.' Hilary got up. 'Do you mind if I switch the radio off?' Before Faith could reply she had switched off the power. Silence flooded the room.

'That's better. I can never think properly with the radio on.' Hilary sat down again. Faith sighed and closed her eyes. Hilary never did have any real feeling for music, she seemed impervious to it. So odd really, Faith thought, when she had heard it throughout her childhood. Faith would have liked to drift off to sleep but Hilary's quiet voice persisted.

'Joss and I would like you to come back to England. We don't want you so far away.'

Faith opened her eyes.

'You mean some sort of nursing home?' she asked guardedly.

'No, I don't. It would be possible for you to come and live with Winnie and me.'

Faith made a sudden movement as if she wanted to sit up.

'Oh I couldn't do that! What an invasion of your privacy. What a liability. Anyway what would happen during the day when you're both at work?'

'Arrangements could be made. There are more services in London than there are here. With Winnie working in the social services she knows all that's available and how to get it. You know how big our flat is. You could be on the ground floor at the back, giving onto the garden.'

At that moment the telephone by Faith's bed rang. It was Jocelyn. By the time Hilary passed the receiver to her mother, Faith's other daughter had been put fully in the picture.

'Mum, you must come home. We can't bear to have you so far away.'

'I'll think about it, darling,' was all that Faith would say.

Afterwards Faith heard Hilary go out on the terrace and pace up and down, smoking her last cigarette before going to bed. She had always been a heavy smoker and Faith thought that she had smoked even more during this past week.

Faith was now wide awake, sleep having been successfully banished for the better part of the night. She shrank into the shell of her shrivelled body like an alarmed snail within its carapace. If only she had gone on swimming that morning along the shaft of sunlight. Out ... out ... out to sea, to have her stroke and quietly drown in the still, deep water of that perfect morning. *Stop deluding yourself, you old fool – you would have died in panic, threshing about with your unaffected limbs, desperately trying to keep afloat, choked by your childhood terror.*

Faith moved her good arm and coiled it round the top of her head on the pillow. Fantasy is fantasy and reality is reality, she thought, and when the two meet, how do we disentangle them? If dead she could no longer hear The Creation; if dead she could no longer commune with her thoughts as she was now doing.

But to return to England, to London, to Kilburn. To leave forever this translucent light, this limpid sea, this house she has built and made her home – what pain, what loss! But life is stippled with loss.

And my independence? she thought. What independence? the dark room wafted back to her. In reply she moved her right leg defiantly beneath the sheet, a self-deprecating grimace wrinkling her face in the darkness. With her good arm she fumbled beneath the sheet for the paralysed one, gripped it by the wrist and raised it up in the air. Then she let go. It fell with a thud on the bed. What price my independence now? she had asked herself.

Maria comes back with Faith's cardigan and helps her put it on. They look at one another. Faith smiles and Maria bursts into tears. Faith pats Maria's hand which rests on Faith's paralysed arm.

'Don't cry, Maria. It could be worse.' Maria nods and fumbles in her pinny pocket for her handkerchief. She blows her nose noisily and wipes her face. Every now and again her Latin temperament gets the better of her and emotions well up to the surface. Especially now she knows she has been absolved from any future responsibility. That Faith is to go to England is a matter for sorrow but not unmixed with relief.

Maria goes back to her mopping and Faith contemplates the letters laid out before her. She picks one up and puts it down again. Thoughts pursue one another across her brain. A dominant image hovers at the forefront.

The room had been full of mourners, friends and relatives who had returned to the house from the crematorium. Faith cut swathes between them as she handed out cups of tea and neatly cut sandwiches. It had rained almost solidly for two weeks and the roads had been greasy with mud washed down from the hedgerows. Mud-bespattered cars were parked in the yard and their owners had plunged through great puddles to get to the house.

Morgan had died in hospital where he had been transferred for a second operation which had proved useless. Forty-two years old, his life had been truncated by a cancer which did not respond to treatment.

As she moved among the people present, Faith felt lightheaded and she imagined she swayed as she walked. She could hear herself talking (too much, she thought) in a voice that wasn't quite her own; it seemed higher pitched somehow, and urgent. She felt she was two persons really, a silent, withdrawn Faith who was manipulating the strings of the other like a puppet master.

Every now and again her path crossed with Oliver who had prepared all this food.

'How are you bearing up?'

'I'm not.' And she moved away, manipulating her puppet self.

She looked around for the girls. Jocelyn, rising thirteen, was chubby with her father's thatch of black hair. She was talking to her favourite uncle, Morgan's half-brother who had come from north Wales for the funeral. Her usually pink complexion appeared red and blotchy, her dark blue eyes creased up into narrow slits. Nearly all the relatives were Morgan's.

He had come from a vast family with many ramifications. All Faith could muster were a few cousins whom she rarely saw. Her mother was still alive but too frail to travel.

Where was Hilary? She should really be here to help me, Faith thought irritably. There was no sign of her about the house.

During those last two weeks when Morgan had been in hospital, Hilary and Jocelyn had been looked after by their neighbours who were also close friends. After an initial visit, Hilary had refused to come any more to see her father in hospital, whereas Jocelyn had clamoured to visit more often than Faith felt advisable because of the pain it caused her. When told of their father's death, Hilary had gone out on her bicycle; Jocelyn had sobbed inconsolably in her mother's arms.

People began to melt away and soon Faith had shaken the last consoling hand and accepted the last sympathetic embrace. They were all gone, except for Oliver.

'I can't thank you enough for all you've done today.'

'It was the least I could do,' he replied.

Oliver and Morgan had been friends since university. Oliver, a tall man, lean and smooth, lived in nearby Bath with his old but still active mother. He had been a consistent visitor to their house since they moved there, just after Hilary was born. Both architects, the two men sometimes combined on work but it was basically a personal friendship.

One day Faith had asked her husband why he thought Oliver had never married. Morgan had shrugged and said, 'I dunno. Only son, only child, stuck with a possessive mother. I should think she'd be enough to frighten off any potential wife. She's a fierce old thing.'

'Seems a pity. He's got a good job and he's so good looking.'

'Yes, well ... He's a bit of a loner,' Morgan had replied. 'Not the marrying type.'

'I'll leave you now, Faith,' Oliver said, planting a kiss on her forehead. 'I'm sure you want to be alone with your daughters. Phone me if I can do anything.'

Oliver was always on the formal side. Faith never felt she could exhibit too much emotion in front of him. She heard his car reversing in the yard and the sound of the engine diminishing as he drove down the lane. She went into the kitchen and as she did so the back door opened and Hilary appeared in a wet mac and wellington boots.

'Hilary, where *have* you been? I looked for you everywhere. You just disappeared after we got back.'

'I went for a walk. I couldn't stand all those people.'

'They were our friends and family. It was very odd of you not to be there. I could have done with some help.'

'You had Joss and Oliver.' The rain ran off Hilary's uncovered head, causing her wet hair to hang in rats' tails around her pinched white face.

'That's not the point. And don't stand dripping all over the floor. Get changed and come and help me clear up.'

'Leave it, Mum. I'll do it with Joss.'

'No, no. The poor child is washed out by everything.'

'And what about me?' Hilary had by now taken off her wet mac and was vigorously drying her hair with a towel she had taken off the Aga rail.

Faith opened her mouth to say something and then suddenly she was overtaken by sobs. She subsided onto one of the wooden chairs and dropped her head on the kitchen table.

'Oh Mum!' Hilary dropped the towel and came round the table. She sat down on the chair next to her mother and laid her arm round Faith's shoulder.

'You go and lie down. I'll bring you a cup of tea.'

Jocelyn came into the kitchen and Hilary looked up.

'You and I are going to clear up. Mum needs to lie down. Get a tray and start to bring the things through.'

Jocelyn did not reply but did as her sister told her.

'Go on, Mum. Go upstairs,' Hilary persisted. Faith raised her head and patted Hilary's hand which rested on her shoulder.

'I think I will.'

That night in the empty bed Faith lay and listened to the rain gushing through the hole in the guttering outside the bedroom window. In a mental aside she noted fleetingly that she must get it seen to. Odd practical thoughts darted in and out of the mainstream of her reflections.

Mismanaged – everything she had mismanaged. The funeral: the girls: it had all been too much. Events had overwhelmed her by their own volition. She had been taken over: she had lost control.

Although Morgan had not been a militant atheist and did not try to demolish the religious belief of others, he was totally impervious to any proselytising. There was no God and all religions were man-made institutions which at different times in history had wielded colossal political power and were always an instrument of social control. To Morgan, religion was divisive, and although he acknowledged that it could show compassion and love, he believed it was more often hypocritical and cruel.

'The Vicar says he will bury Daddy.'

This was Hilary's announcement to her mother when she returned from her cycle ride on the day of her father's death.

'Daddy is to be cremated,' was Faith's reply. Hilary had turned without a word and left the room. Faith knew she should have gone after her, tried to comfort her. But she found Hilary so difficult, so unreachable. Prickly and introverted.

As Faith had sat by Morgan's hospital bed during those

last days when he was no longer conscious, she had ideas about arranging a secular funeral for him. But when it came to the point it all seemed too difficult. It was easier to swim with the tide of convention. Oliver did nothing to encourage her.

'Do-it-yourself funerals embarrass people,' he had said. 'Morgan will forgive you for letting the professionals handle it.'

She felt she had failed him. There had been no poetry in his dispatch, only the clockwork efficiency of an impersonal crematorium. Would a village graveside service have been more appropriate? Words he did not believe in would have been uttered by a clergyman of whose mission in life he was sceptical. No, he would probably have hated that.

And now he was gone, rendered to instant dust in the crematorium furnace. In the darkness of the night, Faith's imagination reconstituted from the dust that he now was, the image of the man he had been, unique as we are all unique and equally – universal.

The thick black hair, cropped short like a brush, the expressive brown eyes which could liquify with emotion or sparkle with mischief; the stocky but agile body set on sturdy legs, a little short for good proportioning – the whole packed with a kind of explosive energy. This was the picture she wanted to retain, but it kept being overlaid by the doppelgänger of a sick man.

She felt she had not spent enough time with the girls during these past weeks. All her energy had been taken up with Morgan, with driving to and from hospital. It was only when she had been told that there was no hope that she had brought them home from her neighbour and attempted to reach out to them. With Jocelyn it was easy, she cried endlessly and allowed herself to be comforted. She refused to go to school and Faith did not insist.

Hilary, she could not reach. For two or three years now, ever since she was about twelve, Hilary seemed to have grown away. Faith imagined that it was connected with the religious phase she was going through and perhaps she thought her mother disapproved. But Faith neither approved nor disapproved.

When she had mentioned Hilary's withdrawal to Morgan, he brushed it aside.

'It's her age. She's discovering herself. She's discovered religion and the Vicar is very good-looking. It'll pass.'

And then had come the onslaught of Morgan's illness and everything else got pushed to the periphery.

Faith had found it therefore particularly touching, the concern Hilary showed for her on the evening after the funeral.

Maria has finished her work and is putting away the mop and dusters. Faith, who now holds one of the letters in her good hand, looks up and says, 'It's all right for you to go now, Maria. Hilary will be back soon. I'm all right.'

'I don't like leaving you alone.' As Maria speaks they can hear the sound of a car drawing up at the front of the house. In a few minutes Hilary comes through the arch from the front door laden down with carrier bags. Maria helps her take them to the kitchen and then departs.

'How's the letter reading going? Who are they from anyway, some secret lover?'

'Alas, I never had any secret lovers.'

'What about Charles?'

'He was hardly secret.'

'Well you did disappear for a short period of time.'

Faith smiles. The reminiscent smile of the old.

'Some of these are Oliver's letters.'

'Oh him. I happened to be in Bath about a year ago

and I saw him by chance on the street. At least I think it was him.'

'How did he look?'

'Desiccated.'

'He must be well into his eighties.'

'You should know.'

'Did you speak to him?'

'No. He didn't see me and what could I have said really?'

The Letters

The box contains a mixed assortment of letters and Faith is wondering about many of them, why had she kept them? The only ones of any possible interest to her daughters are the dozen or so Morgan wrote from his various postings during the war. There are the few she received from Charles from the States, an arbitrary selection from various friends, a few drawings from the grandchildren, and the odd postcard, but mainly they are from Oliver. His neat, even handwriting covering pages week after week, expressing the same sentiments. Just to look at them without even reading the content is enough to bring back to Faith that sense of entrapment she felt even after she had left.

Unwillingly she picks one at random and runs her eye down the page: phrases spring out at her: ... *veiled accusations ... in any way treated you badly? ... never compete with Morgan ... if you had 'gone off' with someone...*

She lays the letter down on the table again. She can hear Hilary in the kitchen, preparing lunch. Absently Faith moves the fingers of her right hand round the outline of her paralysed one which rests on her lap. Thirty years on, those phrases can still trigger the memory of the confusion and pain of that period. Perhaps she handled it badly, but how else could she have handled it?

Faith does not want to read any more of these letters – repetitive, one-track and wilfully obtuse. I should have burned them years ago, she thinks as she drops them back into the box. Emotional as well as physical debris should be got rid of. With her one hand Faith manoeuvres her chair towards the open glass doors giving onto the terrace. Maria has knotted the bead curtains to each side so Faith has a clear view across the ruffled water to the far horizon. Life is not like knitting which can be unravelled to correct a mistake or pick up a dropped stitch. No, Faith thinks, it is more like the fabric she used to weave on her loom, the warp already threaded at birth and the weft constructing life's pattern. *Mine is nearly complete: sober colours shot with brilliant patches: there are areas of plainness (soft greys and greens) and round the edge a reassuring band of blue. Its patterns are zigzags, straight lines and circles, most of all circles.* Faith stares out to sea and observes on the uneven surface of the water, the fabric of her days and years. She sees colour, patterns – no definite overall design – but drab it is not.

It is now just over fifteen years since Charles left her. She had been at the end of her fifties and the blow had been at first crippling and, in a sense, deeply frightening. She had grown used to thinking of herself as being accompanied (bar unforeseen accidents) for the rest of her life. Charles had been ten years younger and it was unlikely that he would die before she did. His desertion was one more loss to add to the others, but devastating though it was she did not fall apart. Even at the height of her unhappiness she had known in an obscure, intuitive way that somehow she would surmount the difficulties.

She and Charles had built Piedras as a sort of romantic odyssey, which bound them together and kept them together for probably longer than would have been the case had it not existed. Houses had always held a fascination for Faith and in her time she had bought up derelict houses in England, converted and sold them for a tidy profit.

Building the villa had also been, at one level, an exorcism. Marriage to Oliver two years after Morgan's death had been a hideous parenthesis which could neither be plucked out of her life nor resolved and laid to rest. She had left Oliver several months before meeting Charles but she still remained enmeshed in the web of his blind persistence, in the shape of his weekly letter.

'Why don't you get divorced from that old queer,' Charles had said. 'Then we can get married.'

'He won't divorce me.' Later, when the law changed, she took the necessary action herself. By then she and Charles had been together for ten years and he was no longer particularly interested in marriage.

Her flight had been not only from Oliver as a person but from all the greyness that went with him. The grey streets, the grey rain and the grey, cold atmosphere which had reigned inside that grey, stone house, where the lines of communication had become ossified like striae on rock. To burst into the Mediterranean light enveloped in the exuberance of Charles' early passion had been a phoenix-like rejuvenation. A release so powerful as to obliterate everything and everyone not immediately concerned in her delirious present. Her daughters were to lose track of her (literally) for several weeks. When she surfaced again (came to her senses some might say) their lives too were changing.

'Shall we eat inside or on the terrace?' Hilary has come out of the kitchen. She does not receive an immediate reply. Faith has half-heard the question, but her mind is elsewhere.

'Mother where do you want to eat?'

Faith backs her chair away from the window and turns it round to face Hilary.

'There's no sun today, I think it's a bit chilly on the terrace.'

'All right. I'll lay the lunch in here.' Hilary takes the box off the table. 'What's to do with these?'

'There are a few wartime letters from your father you may want to keep. The rest can go in the incinerator. They're mainly from Oliver. I can't think why I kept them for so long.'

'Guilt perhaps?'

'Why do you say that?'

'Well you left him, didn't you?'

'That doesn't make me automatically guilty. Anyway you know I'm against guilt. It's corrosive and unproductive.'

'He was just rather a pathetic creature, that's all. Sad really.'

'Most misfits are pathetic.'

'I'm not pathetic.'

'Who said you're a misfit?'

'Well you know what I mean. He was homosexual and I'm a lesbian. Neither of us in the general stream of things.'

'You've made your life constructively.'

'I'm a different generation. And don't forget it was a criminal offence when you were married to Oliver.'

'Well ... it's all water under a very old bridge now. Let's have some lunch.'

Wartime England – Faith and Morgan with their two small daughters: Hilary, three years; Jocelyn, a few months. The war was drawing to its close. Only the atom bombs on Japan were yet to fall. Living as they did in rural Wiltshire, the war made few direct inroads into their life. Morgan had managed to get his call-up deferred until after Hilary was born, owing to a government project his firm was involved with, and although it was curtailed by the war it was not cancelled. Thereafter, as a sapper, he succeeded in staying mainly within the county and managed to avoid overseas postings, not unaided by an inflamed appendix which led to peritonitis. Morgan had vaguely pacifist leanings, but once started, he felt the war must be won.

Unlike some, to whom their wartime service gave them an excitement and purpose lacking in their civilian life, Morgan couldn't get back to civvy street quickly enough. During the war his main object had been to stay alive. He experienced no desire for either military glory or promotion. Although he resisted pressures to apply for officer status, he did finish the war as a sergeant.

Faith, for her part, felt she had been so lucky. She had seldom suffered anxiety on Morgan's account and if rationing and transport problems were irksome, one became accustomed. Living in the country it was easier to come by scarce foodstuffs like eggs and butter. So she cared for Hilary, grew large quantities of vegetables and donated what time she could to certain local organisations in order to feel that she was 'doing her bit'. But the real war was 'way out there' and impinged little on her personal life.

She was overjoyed when Morgan was demobbed, and because he had never been really that far away and had managed to get home for short leaves on a fairly regular basis, they were spared the problems of adjustment which were the lot of so many couples when the war ended.

When reconstruction began, Morgan had more than enough work. Faith, having been left a legacy by an uncle, invested it in a broken-down cottage which she converted and successfully sold. This was the start of an activity which she was to carry on intermittently throughout most of her life. When the girls were young she found it was work she could satisfactorily combine with her domestic obligations. She enjoyed poring over estimates, she was good at battling with the council and getting the maximum of any grants available. She became expert at maximising the potential of any property she bought, without going over the top, and she managed her builders with tact and firmness. They knew they could not mess her about but they did not resent her. Gradually she built up a useful little capital sum which was to stand her in good stead in the years to come.

But the trouble with Faith was that she became attached to the cottages she converted and often 'took against' the people who wanted to buy them. They were not the sort of people she wanted in 'her' cottages! Morgan had been understanding. He never tried to intrude his own very acute business sense with a male superiority as many men might have done.

'It's your creation,' he would say. 'You've lived with it, struggled with it and know it intimately. But you've really done it to make some profit and if you don't sell it to whoever has the money you won't be able to go on to your next one.'

Faith had laughed and replied, 'I know, I know.'

The sale would go through. Faith could be dreamy but basically her feet were on the ground. Occasionally the reverse would happen. She would take a great shine to certain people. They were just right for a particular property but they did not have quite enough money, so she would drop the price. When later she told Morgan, somewhat shamefacedly, he would purse his lips, raise his eyebrows and then say with a tolerant smile, 'It's your house.'

Time passed in that seemingly uneventful manner of a smooth and regularly revolving family life. It was a home and family centred existence which seemed to suit them both. When restrictions were lifted they went to France for their holidays, mainly motoring and camping with stop-offs to look at churches and chateaux for as long as the girls' attention span would allow.

Morgan was a good father. He took a real interest in his daughters and went out of his way to answer their questions and play games with them. But it was fairly obvious that from quite an early age Hilary was his favourite – no doubt, Faith thought, because she was their firstborn. As Hilary grew older, he would take her out on her own to museums and galleries with the excuse that Jocelyn would be bored. When Faith one day pointed out to him this apparent favouritism, he reacted with surprise.

'You think I favour Hilary?'

'Yes, a bit too obviously.'

'Well it's not intentional, I assure you. I love little Jocelyn every bit as much.'

There followed a period when he obviously made a conscious effort to be more even-handed but very gradually he slipped back into his old ways.

Morgan used to take his daughters to school by car. Or, to be more precise, he took Jocelyn to where the school bus picked her up for the village school, while Hilary, who was now in her second year at a grammar school in the town where her father worked, he drove to the school gates. In the afternoon Faith cycled to pick up Jocelyn where the school bus dropped her off, and Hilary on most days came back on public transport which left her with a short walk home, occasionally she would wait for her father and be driven back.

Faith had started evening classes in weaving twice a week and on those evenings the minute Morgan got home she would get into the Citroën and drive off to her class. Morgan and the girls would get their own supper and Faith had no doubt that Morgan allowed himself to be persuaded into letting the girls stay up later than normal, watching television. They had only very recently installed one and it was still quite a novelty.

On one evening Faith arrived at the college to find that the class had been cancelled because the instructor was off sick. She went to visit some friends, chatted and drank coffee with them but arrived back home earlier than normal. She walked into the sitting room where Morgan was sitting on the sofa with Hilary on his knee. Dislodging her abruptly, he got up when Faith entered the room.

'You're back early.'

'Yes, there was no class. I dropped in to see Rose and Tony. Hilary you should be in bed by now.' Faith looked at Hilary who stood between her parents, her face slightly flushed and her eyes dimmed with apparent sleepiness.

'It's not that late. We'd just turned off the box.' Morgan's voice had a slightly defiant note, as if he were the child rather than the parent.

'Off you go, Hilary,' said Faith and Hilary slipped out of the door.

'No sense of time, darling, have you?' said Faith kissing Morgan lightly on his cheek.

Morgan had not responded to this remark with his usual good-natured flippancy. He turned away from his wife and moved towards the door.

'I'm tired. I'm going to bed,' he said over his shoulder as he left the room.

Faith twitched a few cushions and turned out the sitting room lights. She went through to the kitchen and turfed the cat out into the darkness. When she went upstairs the landing light was still on. In Hilary's room she could just make out the outline of her head on the pillow.

'Goodnight, Hilary,' she said, bending to give her a kiss. With a convulsive movement Hilary pulled the sheet over her head.

'Go away,' she growled. Faith drew back, startled. Then

she shrugged – presumably this was the onslaught of adolescence.

In their own bedroom, Morgan appeared to be asleep. He must have been very tired, he was rarely asleep before she was and never this early. When Faith slid into bed she felt very wide awake. Snuggling up close to Morgan she listened to his breathing. She did not think he was asleep.

'Morgan ... darling?'

'Mm.'

'Are you awake?'

'Not really.'

'Don't you want to talk?'

'No.'

'Anything else?' She drew her hand tentatively down his thigh.

Morgan did not reply and turned away from her. Faith lay open-eyed on her back and sleep was a long time in coming.

It was not long after this that Morgan's cancer was diagnosed.

Faith is watching the faces of her daughters as they converse. On Hilary's pale skin and fine features, that set look of middle age from which there is no going back, is already hovering. Jocelyn you might still place in her thirties if you did not know her true age. In her chubbier features there persists the aura of youth, and it is only in her slightly thickening figure that middle age can be detected.

'I don't mind getting to the airport early,' Hilary is saying, 'because then you'll be back shortly after Maria leaves. That won't leave Mother so long alone.'

'I'll be all right,' Faith says.

'Yes, I know you will, Mum.' Jocelyn makes an effort to smile at her mother. She had arrived yesterday to take over from Hilary, who is returning to London. She last saw her mother in the early summer, and is appalled and saddened to see her shrunken and huddled in her chair and to watch her restricted, clumsy movements. Only when Faith speaks and Jocelyn closes her eyes, can she remember her mother as she used to be. The voice is the same; her faculties are still intact. By not looking, Jocelyn can blot out the image of the helpless old woman that her mother has become.

Although Hilary has been scrupulously careful to include Faith in all the planning, Faith nevertheless feels herself like a parcel being disposed of. Should it go there or here? Which would be the best route? She feels she is an inanimate object, which of course in a way she is. But she is grateful to be allowed the semblance of some control.

'But I can't come and live with you and Winnie,' Faith has expostulated again and again. Not because she herself is appalled at the prospect but because she is fearful what her presence may do to the lives of her daughter and her friend.

'Look, Mama, I have discussed it all with Winnie and she *wants* you to come. We don't live in a two-roomed flat. You know how fond she is of you. In fact I think she regards you in some ways as the mother she never had.'

This has been an ongoing conversation between Hilary and Faith but now it is finally resolved and accepted. Hilary is going back to London to arrange for some practical adjustments in the flat and prepare things for Faith's arrival. Jocelyn has come to stay with her mother until Hilary returns for the final move.

'Come on, Joss, we'd better be going.' Hilary kisses

her mother. 'Be good and don't give Joss too hard a time.' Faith utters a dry little laugh.

Maria is hovering in the kitchen doorway and she comes to embrace Hilary. She attempts to take Hilary's case but Jocelyn has already picked it up and the two sisters leave.

Life After Death

It had been nearly a year since Morgan's death, and Faith was beginning to emerge from the undergrowth of mourning. She was coming out into the open to look about her and take stock of the route ahead. Always supposing that the route did in fact go forward and did not double back on itself, she thought. The supposition that life proceeds in a linear fashion from cradle to grave always seemed rather suspect to Faith. She felt sure it was as often a question of loops and u-turns, and that you could find yourself back at the same point from which you thought you had departed some time ago. Lines or loops? Squares or circles? Whatever form life took, it always held a grain of surprise, an element of the unknown. Curiosity about what the future might hold was one of the submerged driving forces of Faith's life.

But more immediately, in the weeks and months after Morgan's death, it was the everyday structure of the daily routine to which she clung. And there was enough of that to keep her going. More than enough. She sometimes felt resentful that she was landed with all the chores, those which had been Morgan's as well as the ones that had always been her responsibility. The girls helped sometimes, but they were at school and had to study when they came home. Besides, Faith was loath to make too many demands on them.

It was lonely living in the country, and had it not been for her neighbours Faith would have found it very hard to get by. Without Morgan, the country seemed somehow threatening and hostile.

Just before the onset of Morgan's illness, Faith had bought another semi-derelict cottage but had not made any attempt to start the reconversion. It had stood a couple of years or so, unattended and indeed unvisited, deteriorating even more from want of attention. So one day in the early spring she took the cottage key out of her desk drawer and got into her car. She drove in the direction of Bath and a few miles before reaching the town, turned sharp left into a narrow, switchback lane with tall banks on either side. The hedges crowning the grassy banks had just begun to sprout a suspicion of green.

The car nosedived down the last steep switchback to where the landscape flattened out into broad farmland. Clumps of tall elm trees, as yet unsmitten by disease, stood dark and brooding in the middle of big fields where cows and horses grazed. The sky was blue-grey with a tentative sun forcing thin rays through wispy cloud. Faith slowed down by a small bridge and turned right along a narrow cart track which ran beside the small stream – hardly more than a ditch really – enveloped in tangled undergrowth. The cottage stood on a slightly raised piece of ground to her right. The deeds had been unclear as to where the exact boundaries were. A small area of land had been staked out at the time of purchase which more or less coincided with what was indicated on the deeds.

Faith eyed her purchase from the car and was taken aback to see how much it had deteriorated: this red brick cottage; two up, two down, built at the end of the nineteenth century or the beginning of the twentieth, to house some farm labourer's family. She got out of the car and approached the front door up two crumbling brick steps.

Nettles and bramble tentacles swarmed across the lower half of the door and she pulled a few away with her gloved hands. The key turned quite easily in the lock but she had to put her shoulder to the door in order to open it. The stairs ran almost directly up from the front door, there being only just room to close it and turn around in the tiny square which served as a hall. Faith went into the larger of the downstairs rooms which led through to a lean-to at the back where there had been a primitive kitchen. The cracked window panes were covered in cobwebs and when Faith ran her finger across one of the murky panes a small triangle of glass fell out and shattered on the floor.

Upstairs in the two bedrooms the greasy wallpaper was peeling off the walls, the pattern of clustered rosebuds faded and discoloured. She peeled back a section of drooping wallpaper and several grey woodlice scurried out. Faith stepped back, repelled by these unattractive creepy crawlies. She looked out of the window, bending her head slightly to do so and saw the green farmland unfolding in a generous sweep to meet the skyline.

She went back down the stairs which were as solid as the broad oak planks in the upstairs rooms. It was only downstairs where the rising damp, in the absence of a damp course, had wrought havoc so that the floors would have to be replaced. Outside, Faith walked around the cottage, pausing to close the door of the ramshackle wooden shed which housed the earth closet. Then she returned to the car, and backing it out onto the main lane, she set off for home.

She felt some affinity with the dismal state of the cottage. She too had been broken down, shrouded in emotional cobwebs and covered in the dust of repetitive daily routine. Since Morgan's death the sparkle had gone out of life. It was not that life was hopeless (her daughters gave her incentive) but she felt it to be limping along, seriously impaired by the difficulty of putting together the broken bits. Their life had been lived very much interlaced, and it took Faith some time to disentangle the skein, to discover the individual strands and to separate out what was now hers from what had been Morgan's; to move from a shared viewpoint to an individual one.

As she drove through the tepid sunshine she thought that if she started to renovate the cottage it might help her to renovate herself. She glanced at her watch, and then instead of taking the turning for home, she continued along the main road towards Bath.

Oliver's office was near the centre of the town and Faith made her way there from the car park. The firm's secretary knew Faith quite well and always treated her sympathetically.

'Mr Norton is in a meeting at the moment but he shouldn't be long. Will you wait or would you like to come back?'

'No, I'll wait,' said Faith. The secretary handed her the daily paper. Faith settled herself on the sofa and turned the pages in a desultory manner.

Oliver had been so much help to her in practical matters after Morgan died. Faith did not really know how she would have managed without him. She was not an impractical person, but so exhausted was she by the strain of her husband's illness that after his death she was overcome by an inertia so powerful it allowed for only the smallest of physical actions (such as getting dressed) and even smaller decision making – whether to have tea or coffee. For a time she could not handle anything larger or more complex. She did not have to, Oliver was always there. But if ever she tried to engage his attention on aspects other than the practical, he shied off. She could never get him to talk about Morgan except in the most oblique way and any indication of her own emotions embarrassed him acutely.

She turned the pages of *The Times*, glancing at the headlines but reading little of what lay beneath. Then she saw Oliver emerge from his office, accompanied by a prosperous-looking couple. Oliver showed them out before greeting Faith, although he acknowledged her presence as they passed by where she was sitting.

'Well this is a nice surprise,' he said as he sat down on the sofa beside her. 'Just in time for lunch.'

'Is it that late already? I must have spent longer the cottage than I thought.'

'What cottage?'

'One I bought just before Morgan became ill. Actually I came to ask you for some advice about it.'

'Let's talk about it over lunch. Where would you like to go?'

'Where do you usually go?'

'A rather smoky pub round the corner. But there's a nice little restaurant near the Roman baths, let's go there.'

And so something which had started spontaneously soon developed into a regular weekly occurrence. Faith slipped into the habit of lunching once a week or so with Oliver after her inspections of the building progress at the cottage. Oliver had recommended to her a small independent builder to replace the one she had used so successfully before but who had now emigrated to Australia. When she encountered problems she would raise these over lunch and Oliver would give his opinion and offer suggestions. One day at lunch, after one such discussion (it had something to do with repositioning the stairs), Faith had laughed and said, 'I really am the limit, picking your brains and getting advice that most people pay a hefty fee for.'

'I enjoy giving advice, especially as you can't come back at me if I'm wrong! But I must say I would like to have a glimpse of this little property sometime, though I have a fair idea from your description what it's like.'

'Well why not? I didn't suggest it because I thought it might bore you. Perhaps I might pick you up in my car one day and run you over there, and then take you to lunch at the village pub which is pleasant enough and has a nice garden to sit in if we get a good day.'

'That sounds like a nice idea.'

It was the first week in June that Faith took Oliver to look at the cottage. A mild, sunny day – they were able to sit in the pub garden afterwards drinking lager and eating what the pub was pleased to call a Ploughman's Lunch. There had been no work going on at the cottage because, in the manner of so many small builders, the workmen had been sent off on another job deemed more urgent. But Faith had become accustomed to the stop/go schedule of small firms and so long as there was more go than stop it did not faze her. It had all looked fairly chaotic with rubble heaped outside and fresh building material stacked for use. But at least the floorboards downstairs had been removed and fresh joists were in position ready for the new floor to be laid.

'You'll be able to sell it as a weekend cottage, but it is a bit too bijou to be thought of as a permanent residence.'

'Yes, I expect so. Though someone might buy it to retire to?'

'Too far from the shops. The retired want convenience.'

'I expect I'll sell it to someone.'

'Oh yes, you'll sell it all right, but you may not have left yourself a very good margin of profit. Why don't you try buying something in a town next time, something bigger? How does the idea of converting a house into flats grab you?'

'It doesn't. It's too big and beyond my scope. I haven't got the experience. I prefer to stick to country cottages.'

'I might be interested in coming in with you on such a project. You know, on a business footing. Think about it. It could be amusing and – profitable.'

'Oh I think I'm safer to stick to small properties. As I said, I haven't got that much experience.'

'That's where I come in. You've got the time to oversee and do the donkey work, which I wouldn't be able to do, but I've got the experience and the contacts.'

'You've done so much to help me with one thing and another, Oliver. I do appreciate it. I'll think about your suggestion.'

'I'm very glad to have been able to help Morgan's widow in any way.' As he said this, Oliver looked past Faith at the sheep, grazing in the field next to the pub.

It was not until she was driving home, after dropping Oliver off at his office, that the peculiarity of the phrase he had used struck Faith. Why hadn't he used the simple pronoun 'you'? It was as if by referring to 'Morgan's widow' he objectified her, gave her a category which blocked out her essential self. She found it odd and vaguely disturbing.

Faith realised, when she thought about it in any depth, that she was quite keen on Oliver. He had a calm assurance and seemed totally dependable, very unlike Morgan's volatile and erratic temperament. But his startling conventional good looks did not seem to fit him somehow. It was as if he were wearing a suit of borrowed clothes. It sounded absurd to say that someone's looks were not part of them but Faith couldn't think of a different description. They seemed to her to be separate, like a suit of armour, and not an integral part of the man. It endowed him with a faint air of mystery which Faith found intriguing.

She had never been to his house and he talked hardly at all about his domestic life. She knew that his mother was now very old and partially infirm but although he occasionally referred to 'my mother' in the course of conversation, Faith had no picture whatsoever of their life together. Any attempt on her part to obtain a more in-depth perception of the day-to-day problems was always deflected. Oliver had nothing to unburden – or so it seemed.

By now both her daughters were at the same secondary school and could travel to and from on public transport. Faith was spared the chore of fetching and carrying which gave her a greater sense of freedom.

Jocelyn seemed to have come to terms with her father's death. Now and again something would trigger off her emotions and she would have a good cry. She was by temperament a happy child, who was popular at school and preferred to go around in groups. Hilary, on the other hand, went in for intense friendships. Where Jocelyn had friends, Hilary always had a 'best friend'. This best friend might change but there would always be one. It was not that she was actively unsociable, but she was more selective than her sister.

Hilary guarded her privacy ferociously and spent a lot of time in her room with the door closed, unlike Jocelyn who was always in and out of the kitchen, the sitting room and, in fine weather, the garden. If she was in her room the door was nearly always wide open, or at least ajar.

Faith had no problems with Jocelyn. For the most part they had an easy, friendly relationship, ruffled now and again by the clash of wills and stormy adolescent flouncings out of the room. But Jocelyn recovered quickly and calm was usually soon restored. Hilary was a different kettle of fish. She and her mother did not argue, did not have rows, but Faith felt shut out by Hilary. She was in no way hostile and, being that much older than her sister, she often showed a more adult concern for her mother's well-being, but it was a detached concern with seemingly minimal emotional content.

Only once did Faith discover Hilary in a state of emotional distress. She had been going to bed one night and as she passed Hilary's room she heard the sound of frantic sobbing. Faith hesitated on the landing outside the closed door; had it been Jocelyn sobbing she would not have felt so hesitant. She listened as she hesitated and when there came a slight pause in the paroxysm, she quietly opened the door.

'Hilary? Darling, what's the matter?'

No reply had come from Hilary and Faith made her way across the room, lit only from the landing light. She sat on the end of Hilary's bed.

'Are you crying about Daddy?'

'Of course I am,' came the angry reply. 'He's in hell and I pray for him every night.'

'Why do you think he's in hell?'

'He was an atheist and a sinner.' Hilary had stopped sobbing and was sniffling into her pillow. Faith saw a box of tissues on the floor beside the bed. She pulled out two and handed them to Hilary.

'He didn't believe in hell. Or heaven for that matter. And after all, aren't we all sinners?'

'That won't help him,' said Hilary, blowing her nose.

'For many people hell exists here on earth and some of us have experienced intermittent glimpses of heaven. They're concepts rather than tangible actualities.'

'What's a concept?'

'An idea. Heaven and hell don't exist as real places, they're more like states of being.'

'How do you *know*?'

'I don't but I have an instinctive feeling.'

'Then where do you think Daddy is now?'

'In my memory. In your memory. In Joss's memory. In the memories of everyone who knew him and still remember him.'

'I don't believe you.'

'You don't have to. I'm just saying what I think.'

'People have to *go* somewhere when they die.'

'Not necessarily. They can just cease to be. Return to primal energy.'

'You say that because you have no faith.'

'No, I have no faith, in spite of my name. At least I have no faith in the sense you mean, orthodox religious faith.'

'What other sorts of faith can anyone have?'

'Plenty. But it's a sort of faith which comes through experiencing life. Something that comes from within and not imposed by external authority.'

'Don't you worry about what is happening to Daddy's soul?'

'No, because I don't quite know what is actually meant by the word – soul. I worry about you and Joss not having a father and I worry about whether I am adequate as a parent.'

'Do you miss Daddy?'

'Of course I miss him. I miss him terribly.'

'But you just carry on as if nothing had happened.'

'That's just what you see on the surface. Like you go to school every day. But we all have things going on beneath the surface. We live our lives at all sorts of different levels. Somehow we just have to carry on. Daddy wouldn't have wanted us to do otherwise.'

'How do you know?'

'I can't *know*, but I can make a fairly good guess.'

'He might have wanted our entire lives to be turned upside down. He might have died so that we should never know a moment's peace. He might have died so he wouldn't have to explain.'

'Explain what, Hilary? I think your imagination is getting the better of you. Daddy died because he had cancer. He didn't want to die but the cancer killed him.'

'Yes I know that.' Hilary sounded impatient. 'But you say we live at different levels so why shouldn't people die at different levels?'

'Because the living are alive but death is irrevocable. To us in this world it has only one level – to extinguish.'

'But I think that death in this world is rebirth in another and if you haven't made amends for your sins in this world they drag you down in the next.'

'Well that's where you and I think differently. It's not for me to try and change your beliefs, but perhaps time will alter them or at any rate make them less worrying to you. Daddy was no more of a sinner than the rest of us.'

Hilary did not reply and they remained quiet together in the semi-darkness. Then Hilary turned over on her side and pulled the bedclothes up around her.

'I want to go to sleep now.'

Faith got up and stooped to kiss the top of Hilary's head which was all that was visible.

'Goodnight, darling. Try not to worry. Things should get easier as time goes on.'

As she lay wakeful in her own empty bed, Faith sent out a silent prayer to a God in whom she did not believe but hoped might be there. But even if he were, out of all the great agonies in the world why should he pay the slightest attention to her, by cosmic measure, minuscule agony? It made no sense.

She turned from God and addressed Morgan instead. *Why are you not here to cope with Hilary? Your favourite daughter who I find so hard to approach. She thinks you're in hell. Are you? Why should she think this? What grounds have you given her other than your atheism? With what ideas did you fill her head when you took her out to museums and picture galleries? Come back, come back and help me. Why should I be left to do everything alone?*

When Faith had called in vain on both God and Morgan, she fell back on her own resources. She put on the light and looked at the time – it was nearly 2 am. She got up and padded quietly down to the kitchen where she made herself a cup of tea. As she sipped it, leaning against the Aga rail and assimilating the warmth from the stove, she wondered if she should have a word with the Vicar. He did not seem the type to be a hellfire preacher. He was an educated man and without his dog collar could well have been taken for a stockbroker.

But the next morning Hilary was her usual aloof, composed self and Faith felt it would be better to leave well alone. Hilary would probably be very angry if she felt her mother was interfering and she would definitely see talking to the Vicar as interference.

Fartlek

Hilary has been gone only two days and now the weather has suddenly broken. Faith and Jocelyn are confined inside the villa and the rain lashes down on every side. Maria has been unable to come as the road is flooded. She has phoned earlier to say that she hopes to be able to make it tomorrow.

Faith sits and looks out on the grey, pounding sea and the deserted jetty continuously awash with waves breaking over it. Black, bulbous cloud rolls across the sky and wisps of whitish mist appear and get blown indiscriminately in any direction. Water from the terrace is inclined to seep beneath the glass doors, and Jocelyn has rolled up some old towels and put them along the bottom of the doors to absorb the water.

The weather has cast rather a blight on both Faith and her daughter, although they do their best to dispel it. Unable to move out onto the big terrace, enjoy the sun's warmth and feel the space around her, Faith focuses almost exclusively on her disabilities and all they entail. For Jocelyn, the bad weather has put an end to her swimming and although she is there primarily to look after her mother, she is disappointed. Normally a mid-summer visitor, she has little idea of how unfriendly the Mediterranean can be.

'How long can this sort of weather last?' she asks Faith, as she stands by the wheelchair gazing through the rain-spattered windows at the turbulent sea.

'Days sometimes, but it usually clears up within the

week. Perhaps the sun will shine again tomorrow, but I'm afraid the sea will have cooled down a lot after this rain and it'll probably be dirty.'

'Pity.'

'Yes, I'm sorry. Would you like to play a game of Scrabble?'

'Not particularly. But if you want to.'

Faith knows that Jocelyn has always played games reluctantly. She needs to do things actively, physically. Her home life is one long round of hectic activity. She runs a small antiques business with minimal help, around which she has to fit in her domestic activities with the children and her husband. She has live-in au pair girls but sometimes they are more of a problem than a help, although the one she has at the moment is reasonably reliable. Faith can see that enforced inactivity chafes Jocelyn as much as ever.

It was a mistake to suppose that she might have been glad of even this short respite from her daily round. The demands that Faith makes are not those that Jocelyn finds easy to respond to.

'I suppose you and Hilary played chess,' Jocelyn says as she brings the Scrabble game to the table.

'Only once or twice.' Faith moves her chair a little awkwardly with her one good hand towards the table. 'There's been so much to do sorting things out. Hilary didn't have much time to spare.'

The wheelchair moves more swiftly than Faith intends, it collides with the table and the slight impact throws her forward on the table, causing her to sweep the box onto the floor. The small white squares scatter across the tiles.

'Now look what I've done!' The vexation in Faith's voice is patent. She pushes with her good arm against the table and regains her sitting posture. 'So clumsy. So inept.'

'Not to worry. They're easily picked up.' Jocelyn crouches down and retrieves the scattered pieces. 'You didn't hurt yourself, did you, Mum? ... You should have waited and let me move you. You're all lopsided the way you are. You can't expect your co-ordination to be brilliant.'

'I don't expect anything to be brilliant. Nothing is brilliant any more, but I'm not going to give up attempting things on my own. Usually I can manage the chair better than that.'

'There, I think that's the lot.' Jocelyn shovels the letters into a small leather bag which Faith keeps for this purpose. Jocelyn shakes the bag up and down then offers it to her mother.

'Go on, pick one.' Faith does so and Jocelyn likewise. They look at their respective letters.

'You start,' says Jocelyn. They pick their seven letters and Jocelyn quickly – with her two hands – has her letters arranged on their little plastic stand and is waiting with simulated patience for her mother to begin.

'I suppose chess is an easier game to play single-handed,' she remarks as she watches Faith juggle her letters around with her active hand.

'Yes, it's one of the few things I don't feel too clumsy at. You never learnt to play, did you?'

'Mike tried to teach me once. But it's so *slow*. I haven't the patience.'

'Hilary always beats me but I think she and Winnie play quite a lot. Is there such a word as "*fartlek*"?'

'I wouldn't think so. It sounds rude to me. Where's the dictionary or has Hilary packed it?'

'No, it's over there on the shelf by the fireplace.'

Jocelyn picks out the dictionary and thumbs through it as she walks back to the table.

'Well, would you believe it there *is* such a word. Its origin is Swedish and it's an athletic term – a method for training long-distance runners, mixing slow with fast work.' Jocelyn closes the dictionary and lays it on the table.

'Oh goody,' says Faith. 'That was sheer luck *and* I get an extra 50 points for laying out all my letters in one go.'

'That gives you a head start. I'll never catch up.'

'Don't begrudge me my small successes. A sheer fluke it was.'

Faith finishes laying out *FARTLEK* on the board.

'Do you think you're going to be all right with Hilary and Winnie, Mum?' Jocelyn is chewing her lower lip as she glances, frowning slightly, from her letters to the board.

'I've no idea. All right is a relative term anyway. How right is all right?'

'Oh Mum, don't talk in riddles. You know what I mean. Are you going to be reasonably content there?'

'I have made up my mind to be as content as I reasonably can in the circumstances. The big hurdle was coming to terms with having to leave here. For the rest, I'll have to take it as it comes.'

'I wish you could have come to us but our house is so impossible, all those stairs and narrow doorways.'

And also, Faith adds silently, your lifestyle. It would have difficulty incorporating such as me.

Always Faith had enjoyed her visits to Jocelyn and Mike at their converted farmhouse in Wiltshire when she had been her autonomous self. But even then, the constant comings and goings of the household, the unruly dogs, the charming and extremely boisterous grandchildren, not to mention the endless draughts because nobody but nobody shut any doors, had irked her somewhat. She was forever furtively booting the cats out of the kitchen and surreptitiously closing the doors. Life might be duller with Hilary, but it would be more comfortable.

'You will miss your friends from around here.' Jocelyn has put her word down and is helping herself to more letters from the leather bag.

'So many of them have gone.' Faith secures a triple word score without a moment's hesitation. 'They've either died or gone back to their respective countries. There's really only my Dutch friends left. You remember the retired engineer and his wife? In the winter I lead quite a hermit's life here, but I've enjoyed it. In the summer, it's different, plenty of people about. But acquaintances really rather than friends.'

'Hilary and Winnie are very together. They seem to have got their life well organised so I am sure they will do their best for you.'

'I know they will. But that's not what I worry about. I'm fearful about how my presence might upset their life.'

'Don't be. They've been together such a long time now and they are secure in each other. They've had no disruptions in their life, like ... having children.'

'Looking after an ageing and semi-paralysed old woman is hardly a substitute for having children.'

'No. But it means they have to focus outside themselves.'

'I wouldn't have called either of them particularly inward looking in the first place.'

'Maybe not. But you know what I mean. Hilary has never been one to give much away. Even when we were girls she kept her cards pretty close to her chest.'

'How do you mean?' Faith contemplates the board and her own letters. The game has become a tight oblong with few possibilities any more. Nothing can be added to with any hope of a decent score.

'You remember after Dad died she was so aloof? Always going off to church and shutting herself in her room. I wanted her to comfort me. Oh you wouldn't understand, she used to say. Understand what? I would reply. Oh go away and don't pester me, was all I ever got. Then when we grew up and I had lots of boyfriends and went to discos and parties, Hilary was off to demos with her girlfriends. It took me some time to realise what it meant and when the penny finally did drop it came as something of a shock.'

Faith manages to add an S to a word and then she looks across at her daughter. She presumes Jocelyn has never known about that other thing – has had no inkling, Faith hopes.

'I've scored four,' Faith says. In whatever way Hilary has achieved it, Faith knows that she has managed to resolve it. Not so for Faith herself. After the shuddering shock of discovery, she had buried it deep and unresolved in those recesses of the mind where the unspeakable resides beneath the cumulative weight of other experiences and events. From time to time throughout her subsequent life seismic heavings in her subconscious had caused this thing to claw its way up to the surface, where she could not bear to examine it and so forced it back down again into the depths. It has not surfaced for some years now but Faith is ever aware that it is – *there*.

'Shall we give up, Mum? It's a hopeless shape and anyway you won easily.'

'That was helped by my spectacular start. *Fartlek* is not a very attractive-sounding word, is it? What did you say it meant again?'

'A method of training runners – fast and slow work across country.'

'You could say that life was a form of *fartlek* – a cross-country run when sometimes we are speeding along with singing hearts and at others the rhythm is so slow and ponderous we almost grind to a halt.'

'It seems to me I'm always in the fast lane.' Jocelyn

gathers the Scrabble pieces together and puts them in the box.

'Well it's the slow lane all the way for me now.' Faith moves her wheelchair away from the table and turns it round so that she can see out of the window. The rain seems less fierce now and there are breaks in the clouds showing, not blue sky, but a paler, less leaden shade of grey.

'I think the storm is blowing itself out. Perhaps tomorrow there will be sunshine again.'

'I hope so.' Jocelyn has put the game away and has come to sit on the chair opposite her mother. 'A spot of sunshine will set me up for the English winter.' Jocelyn gets up again, she can never be still for long.

'I could do with a cup of coffee, Mum. How about you?'

Food and drink are becoming landmarks in the day and Faith, who had never been particularly preoccupied with what she ate, finds herself looking forward to the food others prepare for her and the drinks of various sorts that are brought to her during the day. Is this what one is reduced to, she sometimes wonders, the gratification of bodily needs?

Jocelyn returns with the coffee and pulls up a table on the right of her mother's chair. As she puts down the mug, she says, 'Leave it for a few moments, it's quite hot. But the mug is only three-quarters full.'

This is in reference to the cup of tea yesterday which was scalding hot and full to the brim. As she had brought the cup to her lips, Faith had slopped it down her front. Luckily she had on a fairly thick jersey so the hot liquid hardly penetrated to her skin. Hilary had always been careful how she served the food and drink, but Jocelyn is just getting the hang of it.

Jocelyn sits down on the chair again and curls both

hands around her mug. As she observes her, Faith is reminded of how she used to do the same thing as a child with a mug of cocoa. Not something that Faith can now do. Mentally Faith ticks off her present skills. It is like the so-called milestones of childhood, but in reverse. Skills disappear instead of developing.

'Do you ever wonder, Mum, what made Hilary what she is?'

Faith hesitates. It has been such a very long time since she and Jocelyn have been together in such close intimacy, really not since the first grandchild when Faith went to help in the early weeks just after the birth. Since then, mutual visiting had, in the natural order of things, become family-centred, with Faith organising and planning when they visited her and fitting in when she visited them in England. There was rarely opportunity for quiet chat. She had never discussed Hilary with Jocelyn and never before had Jocelyn raised such a question about her sister.

For Faith it had been the second shock, coming several years after the first one. She had just returned to England after disappearing for several weeks with Charles on his boat. Feeling marginally guilty, she hastened to establish contact again with her two daughters and to reassure them. Hilary had moved into the big Kilburn flat which she said she was sharing with a friend. There would be plenty of room for her mother to stay a few nights.

When Faith showed up, the friend Winnie had been still at work. Hilary was not one to make things explicit, nor was she particularly secretive. She fell back on the use of implication. After showing her mother around the flat, she paused a brief second before opening the last of the doors.

'And this is Winnie's and my bedroom.'

Faith had not immediately taken in the significance of the double bed, feeling momentarily only puzzled that in such a roomy flat they had to share a bedroom. When, shortly afterwards, the possible truth occurred to her, she promptly rejected it. Fresh from her ardent affair with Charles she could not conceive that any daughter of hers could be sapphic. She experienced a sense of almost prudish distaste. But in the days that followed she had no choice but to accept the truth. Almost reluctantly she took an immediate liking to Winnie who, with her dark, curly hair, her faint Yorkshire accent and a ready sense of humour, reminded her of someone. She could not think who. By the end of her visit she had accepted the situation with an internal shrug of quasi indifference (of course her mind was on Charles and how soon she could get back to him).

Then she had gone off to visit her other daughter and meet the man she was intending to marry. Initially she took less of a liking to Mike than to Winnie, but with the years he has mellowed and is less aggressively pleased with himself.

It all seems a very long time ago now. Faith is almost as fond of Winnie as she is of her own daughters, and she has long since accepted the normality of that household.

'I suppose some people are born that way,' was Faith's delayed answer to Jocelyn's question.

'Like Oliver?'

'Like Oliver. I didn't know you knew.'

'Oh *Mum*, how could I not know? It was obvious to everyone except you.'

'Yes I suppose so. But I rather thought you were too young to know, weren't you?'

'We knew a lot more than you gave us credit for.

Besides Hilary confirmed my suspicions after you left him. She said that was why you went.'

'In a manner of speaking ... I suppose, yes. Did Hilary ever tell you anything else?'

'No. Should she have?'

Immediately Faith regretted having asked that question. For years those murky waters had been circumnavigated. What had possessed her, at this moment in life, to sail into them again?

'Is there something else I should have known?'

'No. I just wondered if Hilary had ever talked to you about her own inclination?'

'No, never. You know Hilary. She's never been given to intimate discussion. She ploughs her own furrow. As far as she's concerned if that's the way things are, that's how they are, and other people can like it or lump it.'

Faith moves awkwardly in her chair, trying to settle herself more comfortably, but she only succeeds in dislodging her useless arm which slides dully down towards the ground. Jocelyn gets to her feet and moves to help her mother.

'Leave me,' Faith snaps. 'I can manage.' Laboriously she hauls the offending arm back into position with her good hand. Jocelyn stops in her tracks and her look of pained concern is not lost on Faith.

'I must look pretty grotesque,' she says. 'Sorry I was so snappy but it's irritating.' She laughs bleakly. 'The understatement of all time.'

'Oh Mum I feel so useless.'

'Well you're not. It is I who am useless. As a little girl you always wanted to make things better and I suspect you still do. But there are things in life which cannot be made better and they have to be accepted – endured. We can only limp on.'

At that moment there comes an unexpected break in

the clouds and a shaft of sunlight beams into the room. Jocelyn turns to the window.

'I do believe the weather is changing. Perhaps tomorrow we can get out again.'

But the clouds close in once more to shroud the sun and the only sound in the room is the renewed rain pelting against the glass.

Openings

Faith did not attend the funeral of Oliver's mother. Oliver himself discouraged her.

'You never knew my mother. Her funeral will be very private.'

Faith had felt that the least she could have done was to offer Oliver her support, but he seemed not to require it. However she had been glad to be excused and when they met the day after the funeral Oliver conveyed to her none of his feelings.

By now Faith had successfully sold the cottage and she had embarked with Oliver on converting a Victorian terrace house into three flats. Her girls were growing up and Hilary, newly seventeen, was soon to leave school. She had given up going to church and had become heavily involved in CND. Resisting her mother's efforts to propel her towards university, she said she wanted to take a year out. She and her friend, Anna, were going to travel, were going 'to see the world'.

'And how do you think you're going to finance yourselves?' Faith had asked.

'We can get jobs.' Hilary sounded confident. 'And there's that money Grandma left me.'

Faith had seen that money as a useful reserve to be used perhaps for educational or training purposes. She had been brought up to treat hard-earned savings with respect, to be used for something useful and not frittered away on what seemed to her unproductive travelling. But she knew how stubborn Hilary could be, and if that was what she intended to do, she would do it in the face of all opposition. Oliver was no help when she spoke to him about it. He merely made her feel inadequate that she was unable to dissuade Hilary, and reinforced her fears for Hilary's safety.

'The child should finish her education before she goes gallivanting off. And goodness knows what will happen to her if she gets into the company of all those hippies and layabouts,' was the only contribution he made to the discussions.

In the autumn, after a summer of waitressing and hoarding their pay, the two friends set off. Faith received a series of postcards as they moved slowly through Holland, France and Italy. From Greece, Hilary informed her mother that they were making for Israel and were going to work on a kibbutz.

It was shortly before Christmas that Oliver made his proposal of marriage. They had been seeing each other more frequently since Oliver's mother died. The flats conversion required a considerable amount of consultation and this had spilled over into going for walks at the weekend. With Hilary gone and Jocelyn, at nearly fifteen, frequently out with her mates, Faith often felt at a loose end at weekends and was only too pleased to drive over to Bath and spend part of the day with Oliver. She started going to his house now rather than his office, and on some days when it was too cold and disagreeable to go walking with sandwiches, he would prepare some lunch which they ate in the rather uncomfortable kitchen. Or, if they had been out for an afternoon ramble, he would light the sitting room fire when they got back and give her tea and toast before she went home.

The house was furnished with staid, heavy furniture, some of it antique. The upholstery was mainly red velvet, most of it quite threadbare. The innumerable bobbles and trimmings were in need of renewal. Odd touches of modernity were present in the shape of bookcases and the occasional abstract painting, positioned on the wall next to some sombre oil still life. But those contemporary touches merely served to highlight the incongruity of the whole. It was so different from Faith's own house which was an eclectic mixture of colour and style but which was nevertheless held together by an overall sense of unification. It was, above all, *comfortable*.

Faith had never penetrated beyond the kitchen and the sitting room in Oliver's house. He had a study at the back, at the end of a long corridor, but he had never taken her in there. Neither had she been upstairs, she always used the cloakroom off the hall.

'How long have you lived in this house, Oliver?' she once asked him.

'All my life.'

'All your adult life?'

'No. All my life.'

'You mean you were a child here?'

'Yes. Why do you sound so surprised?'

'It's just a bit unusual nowadays to find someone still living in the house where they were born.'

'I didn't say I was born here. I wasn't. We moved here when I was a year old.'

'Well, give or take a year, it boils down to much the same thing. Did you never leave home?'

'Yes, when I was at university. But Father died when I was fifteen so I had to look after my mother.'

To that remark Faith could think of no adequate response.

It had been a sharp, frosty Saturday in early December and a biting wind had turned them back earlier than anticipated from an afternoon walk. Oliver drew the curtains in the sitting room as the light began to fade, the fire was burning cosily in the grate. Faith unexpectedly had felt herself at home in a way she had never previously experienced in Oliver's house. He had bought crumpets for tea and Faith was toasting them on the end of a long fork before the fire while Oliver made the tea. He carried the tray into the room and sat down on the sofa beside her.

'Pity you have to go home. We could have gone to the theatre this evening.'

'Well actually I don't have to. Joss has gone to an all night party and she won't be back.'

'An all night party? What on earth's that?'

'What I said. A party that goes on all night, or most of the night.'

'And you allow her to go to that sort of thing?'

'I don't have much option. It's the "in" thing and if I were to say no she'd probably go anyway. I'd rather have her cooperation and know where she is and what she's up to. Certainly tonight I have no qualms. I know the parents of the girl who is giving the party and they said they would run Joss home tomorrow.'

'Well then, why don't you stay?'

'I'd like to but I haven't got a toothbrush.'

'Don't worry, I can supply a new one.'

When they got back after the theatre there was still a faint glow in the embers of the sitting room fire. Oliver raked them together and threw on a few small logs. He poured a couple of brandies and they sat sipping them quietly in the soft glow of one lighted lamp and the flickering flames of the burning logs. Faith was on the sofa and Oliver sat on the chair next to the fire. Faith felt vaguely ill at ease, she wasn't quite sure why. It had not been a very good play – a superficial modern comedy which offered little substance for either thought or discussion. An uneasy silence hung between them. Was Oliver going to make love to her? Suddenly Faith had identified the source of her unease. It was not that she viewed such a prospect unfavourably, but she was still confused about her feelings towards him.

It was now two years since Morgan's death and life was beginning to revolve again in more rhythmic motion. Faith felt she was becoming less and less fragmented. But she was not sure whether she was ready to embark on another relationship. Perhaps the whole thing was in her head. Why should he make love to her? He had never shown her the slightest indication of sexual interest. In fact he seemed to go out of his way to avoid touching her. At times, when they crossed a busy road together, when he might have been expected to take her arm, he did not. When once, in the car, she had put her hand on his, he had withdrawn it immediately. He was the least tactile person she had come across. Why then this premonition that he was about to make love to her?

'I expect you would like to turn in now,' Oliver said, poking the fire in an aimless fashion.

'I shall have to be away in fairly good time tomorrow to get home before Joss. So maybe, yes.' Faith rose uncertainly to her feet.

'You know your room.' Oliver looked up at her, the poker held in both his hands. 'I put a toothbrush in the bathroom for you.'

'Thanks. And thank you for the theatre.' Faith stood irresolutely between the sofa and the door.

'Sorry it wasn't a better play.' Oliver had risen to his feet and was standing with his back to the fire, juggling the poker from one hand to the other.

'Well, goodnight then.' Faith turned towards the door.

'Goodnight, Faith.' Oliver sat down again, returning the poker to its place.

Faith went up to her room where she had already made up the bed before going to the theatre. Oliver had handed her sheets and a pillowcase and said, 'I expect you would like to make the bed yourself.'

The room had been bitingly cold (Oliver's house did not have central heating) and the small electric fire, which had been left switched on while they were at the theatre, had barely taken the chill off the room.

On the end of the bed lay a pink nylon nightie. Faith held it up, mild distaste pursing her mouth. She folded it up and placed it on the chair by the window. Not for her Oliver's mother's nightgown. In the bathroom she found the toothbrush and a new tube of toothpaste placed beside it. She wasted little time and was soon between the sheets in her vest and pants. It was cold and she wished she had asked for a hot water bottle.

So much for my presentiment, she had thought, her knees drawn up to her chest and the unfamiliar bedclothes clutched around her in an effort to keep warm. Gradually the warmth of her body percolated the bedding and as the cold receded so she became drowsy and fell asleep.

She did not know what woke her, but when she turned over she saw the door was ajar and a faint light from the landing was seeping into the room. She was about to get up and shut the door, which she presumed she had not closed properly in the first place, when she became aware of a shadowy figure standing at the end of her bed.

In her sleep-confused state, Faith thought she was at home and that it was one of the girls standing there.

'Is there anything the matter?' she enquired sleepily.

'No,' replied Oliver. 'I wondered if I might come into your bed.'

Love-making has many rhythms and Faith knew it would

not be the same with Oliver as it had been with Morgan. She had not been accustomed to making love in the dark, except now and again. Morgan had maintained that lovers should see as well as feel one another, and she was surprised when Oliver shut the bedroom door and immediately switched off the bedside light which she had put on when he got into the bed. But although she was not transported, at least it was no fiasco, and in the posttumescent calm Faith felt a surge of emotion which, if she had been asked to describe it, she might have tentatively labelled love. She was about to draw Oliver close to her again when, to her bewilderment, he kissed her chastely on the forehead, slid out of bed and disappeared from her room.

Why? They were not guilty lovers in a household of prying eyes. His action left Faith puzzled and wakeful, with a sense of having been unjustly abandoned. She wondered in a moment of wild conjecture if perhaps he had been a virgin. But this supposition did not tally with his performance. She knew him well enough to realise that he would be reluctant to reveal much about his previous lovelife. Perhaps it was the fear that she might show an interest in it which had scared him off. Living so long with his mother must have had an inhibiting effect, Faith thought, and she resolved to be patient with his hang-ups and help him to dispel them. On this thought she had turned over and gone to sleep again.

She was woken in the morning by a robust knocking on the door and when she sleepily called out, 'Come in,' Oliver appeared fully dressed and bearing a breakfast tray. He put it down gingerly on the bedside table and then backed away towards the door.

'I thought it would be easier for you to have breakfast in bed.'

'Thank you. What about you?'

'I've had mine. I always get up early.'

'Don't I get a kiss this morning?' Faith sat up in bed, exposing her bare shoulders and breasts.

'I haven't shaved yet. I always fetch the paper first. See you shortly.' Oliver disappeared and closed the door behind him.

How odd, Faith thought, as she got out of bed and switched on the fire. She scrabbled at the bottom of the bed for her vest and pants and then also pulled on her pullover before getting back into bed. She ate the toast thoughtfully and hoped he wasn't regretting last night, because she wasn't. But she had hoped for a somewhat different reaction this morning. Oh well, everyone is different. Patience, she said to herself as she sipped the hot tea and contemplated the situation.

Oliver knocked on the door again but came in immediately before she could reply. He laid the *Sunday Telegraph* on her bed. She caught his hand and held it fast so that he could not draw back.

'I want a kiss, shaven or unshaven.'

Oliver laughed and kissed her quickly on the cheek.

'I hope last night didn't upset you,' he said as he loosened Faith's hold on him and moved towards the door.

'Well hardly. If I hadn't wanted you I would have said so, and presumably you wouldn't have raped me.' With a sudden movement Faith threw back the bedclothes and got precipitately out of bed. She took Oliver by surprise when she flung her arms round his neck.

'I'm very fond of you, you know,' she murmured diffidently.

Oliver held her away from him and looked at her – it was a quizzical look. He placed a careful kiss on her forehead and eased himself out of her embrace.

'And I of you,' he said as he left the room.

It was not until Faith was driving home that the anomalies

of the situation forced themselves on her attention, but she failed to look at them in depth. Instead, they became smothered in suppositions of her own creation, interpreting the situation as she would like it to be interpreted and thus sowing the seeds for future disaster.

She arrived home lighthearted and in good spirits with just enough time to have a bath and a change of clothes before Jocelyn was brought back from the party.

When Oliver finally brought himself round to proposing to her, Faith had already rehearsed the situation. She saw it as the logical outcome of their expanding relationship and although she asked for time to think about it, her decision had already been made. Somewhere, deep down, warning bells sounded, but she did not want to listen to them and they grew fainter as she built up the positive aspects. Oliver was dependable, he was giving her back a sense of security which Morgan's death had dissipated; they had a number of interests in common. Faith did not want to spend the rest of her life alone.

Her main concern had been how the girls would take her re-marriage. In reality it would only be Jocelyn who would be directly affected. Hilary was well on the road to independence and anyway she was out of the country at the moment.

'You mean we'll have to leave this house?' Jocelyn had sounded desolate and Faith realised that the loss of her home was more painful than the prospect of a stepfather.

'Oliver has to be near his work and you'll find there's much more going on in Bath. It'll be far easier to go places. You won't need me to drive you everywhere.'

Gradually Jocelyn came to accept the idea and she was placated by the knowledge that she wouldn't have to change schools.

From the kibbutz in Israel, Faith received a laconic comment: *I suppose you can't mourn Dad forever. Sooner or later this had to happen. Don't worry about me. I have plans for my future. I hope you'll be happy.*

By the time the move took place, Jocelyn was not only willing, but eager to go. She had met a boy at a party. He lived in Bath.

Last Days

The bad weather has moved away. Hilary is back. Jocelyn has gone home. Faith is sitting out on the terrace watching the sunlight sparkle on the ripples of the small waves – they appear to her to give out silver sparks like the sparklers children play with at parties.

Her thoughts chase one another in circles:

Poor Joss, it has been hard for her to come to terms with my condition and although she did her best not to show it, I knew she was greatly relieved to be going back. Back to a life that responds to being organised and put in order as mine no longer can. There's a saying I believe – naturally I can't remember who said it – 'pain were better than tending pain, the one is single the other twain'. Hilary takes me in her stride so much better than Joss, largely I think because she has known pain and confusion and has emerged from it. Joss is more demonstrative but understands less.

How lucky I am that the sun is shining again today and I can be out here on the terrace. That far horizon, this coastline just below me, take me out of myself and I can forget how I am and remember how I was.

Hilary has brought me out my book and I suppose I should read. But it's much easier just to sit and look, and feel with the part of me where feeling still resides – feel the soft breeze on my face and through it, the sun which no longer burns as in summer but is as comforting as a thermal blanket.

Oh damn that useless arm! It's always sliding off the arm rest. Come here, you. I find it hard to grasp and heavy to lift. But yes, I've managed. Up it comes. I'll put it across my knee, maybe under the rug, it always feels so cold to the touch. Increasingly I feel cold, that's why Hilary has put this rug over me, although she's wearing only shorts and a T-shirt. And look, those tourists down there are stripping, they might even swim. Pebble Cove is beginning to look like it does in the winter, all the regulars have moved away. London is not going to be like this, back to greyness, but not *that* greyness. That was in the past and the past is gone. Now there is only the present, no future really, only a present sliding silently into the past.

I am lucky that Hilary and Winnie have a garden, and a really countrified garden, so rare in the middle of London. Am I resigned to leaving? Yes, I suppose so. I adapt. I have had to adapt throughout my life to continue living. Now I have to adapt to die. I would have liked to die here, in sight of the sea. I think I have been happiest here. I was happy with Morgan when I was young and the girls were children, but then... Did *that* invalidate what I thought was happiness – what *was* happiness? What would have happened if I had known when he was still alive?

Better not to ask. I *didn't* know. How is it that you can live with someone and think that you know them intimately, and something happens and you feel that you know them not at all? Mostly I have managed to banish from my thoughts all that I read in Hilary's diary; subsequent life experiences have also insulated me from it.

But from time to time it surfaces and leaves me wondering about this sense of the unknown in someone you once assumed to be a knowable other. Of course I never really pretended to know Oliver with any great intimacy because he made it impossible. Maybe if I hadn't persisted in my search for knowledge I might have accepted the limitations of the marriage and been reasonably content, but I doubt it. But Charles now ... I did think I knew him in the same way I thought I knew Morgan. Then look what happened! I was so cossetted in my security that it seemed unthinkable. Knowing oneself can be equally delusive and I seem to have achieved this only in the past fifteen years. Perhaps that's why I can now adapt to where I am at without too much anger and frustration, though God knows I feel crotchety enough at times.

Sometimes I ask myself whether it is really worth being alive the way I am, and surprisingly enough the answer is in the affirmative. There are still things I enjoy in spite of so many hindrances. Everything has to take its course. I may feel differently when I get to London, when I am, so to speak, on alien territory.

It won't be long now. Last week the estate agent came to take measurements. Some of the furniture, books and pictures have already gone to London, what's left is to be sold with the house. I didn't want to clutter up Hilary's place, but she said she's not over-furnished and that there'd be plenty of room for whatever I wanted to take. In fact she insisted that I must take some of my own things with me. At first I didn't want to bother, it all seemed too much of an effort to decide what to take and what to leave. But I'm glad now that I did do it. It'll be comforting to have some familiar objects round me when I get to London.

I had half hoped that the girls might keep the villa on. But that was impractical of me. After all, it doesn't really mean anything to them. Besides I may need the money. They've been coming here over the years simply because this is where I have lived. I am trying not to think too much how painful it was to have that man from the agency tramping about the place with his metre measure, asking questions, making negative comments so that any positive ones seemed to be cancelled out. I felt an overpowering urge to shout at him, to tell him to get out of my house. How dare he intrude! Then he had this simpering, rather silly little girl with him who wrote things down in a notebook. She kept glancing at me as if I were some sort of freak. I thought ... you wait, my girl ... you too will get old. I'm not usually vindictive, but the whole business upset me. Hilary was so good. She did all the negotiating but always with reference to me. She cut him short when he went rabbiting on. The price he suggested seemed satisfactory enough, a little on the high side but we can always come down. And now the villa has that forlorn look of a home in the process of disintegrating. Part of its contents is missing. There are great gaps on the walls where the pictures have gone. Maria has swept away the cobwebs but the blank spaces remain. The remaining books lie collapsed on the half-empty bookshelves. There is a maimed atmosphere. Indoors that is.

Out here on the terrace I can forget all that. I can sit absorbed in my surroundings, watch the movement of the sea and the changing light on the water. I can almost forget my disability and think myself back as I was. In a few minutes I will get up from my terrace, not my wheelchair, and stroll down to the jetty. I will sit on the edge and trail my feet in the water. It is not warm enough to swim, at least not for me but next summer I'll be in that translucent water again, lying back in its buoyant embrace.

* * *

'Mother, don't you want to read your book?' Hilary jerks me out of my fantasy. She has come out on the terrace and is looking at me with a concern she cannot quite hide. I think she doesn't like to see me looking into space. She likes to see me occupied in some way, and as you can't do much one-handed, reading is about all I can do. I think Hilary fears that when I just sit my mind is a blank, that reading in some way is a therapy for it, will help to keep it reasonably alert and so on. She's right up to a point I suppose. But I have so many thoughts and reflections crowding my mind at the moment, I need to get them sorted. I need to sit and stare.

'I was watching these people down on the jetty,' I say to her. 'Do you think they're going to swim?'

'I shouldn't think so. The water is too cold even for me although the sun is warm. I came to say that your Dutch friends rang. They're off to Holland for a few weeks and they want to come to say goodbye. We'll be gone before they get back. I said to come round this evening for a drink. Is that OK?'

'Yes, I suppose so. I hate saying goodbye. I would just like to go off quietly without any fuss.'

'Small chance of that. You know you'll have Maria and all her family sobbing around you when we leave. You'll have to brace yourself.'

'Yes, you don't have to emphasise it. What I'm saying is that I wish it were all over. I can't stay, therefore I want to be gone.'

'Well we're nearly there. Just be patient a little while longer. At least you'll be seeing the Vanbruyns again, as they tell me they visit London every year. Here, let me find your place in the book.'

Hilary picks up my book from the table and opens it at the book mark. She clips the plastic tray onto the arms of my chair and lays the book down on it, open.

'There you are, have a bit of a read until lunch time.'

Take my mind off things I suppose is what she thinks, I say to myself as I watch Hilary disappear indoors again. Normally I read a lot, it's just that now I am too agitated to concentrate and anyway my concentration is diminishing, at least that's what I suspect. In ten days' time all of this – I mentally raise both hands and indicate the sea, the sky, the villa – will be gone from my life for ever. Could it be that anticipation of loss is worse than the actual loss? Once something has happened you have to come to terms with it, but when you are teetering on the brink everything seems awash beneath your feet.

Perhaps I would feel it less if this plot of land and this house were not so deeply entrenched in the fabric of my life. The excitement of discovering it with Charles that day we sauntered round the coastal path, then so narrow, rough and stony. Now it's wide, smooth and tamed. The For Sale sign had been hung on the fig tree and was so bleached by the sun and weather we had difficulty in deciphering the phone number. Then all the hassles that followed with permits, plans, building delays and so on. All grist to my mill. Calming Charles down when he got over-excited and het up about the delays. Then finally, when it was finished and it had that raw, brash look of the very new and bits of rubble still remained uncleared, the builders vanished and we had to cope with the final tidying up ourselves. As the years passed so it mellowed and matured, as did the garden.

Houses have always played an important role in my life. I've never regarded them as mere buildings, inanimate heaps of brick and mortar. To me they seem to breathe and emanate their own atmosphere. And houses have different meanings for people. For some they are status symbols to show off and entertain in, for others, places to dash back to for food, rest and ablutions from outside engagements, places to come to and leave from but hardly to *be* in. For me this house had become a haven, somewhere to go and shut the door and quite simply abide – in an atmosphere created to suit my particular temperament. If that sounds solipsistic I don't mean it to be. I didn't wish to shut others out but they had to accept what they found and respect my need to be private.

This attitude came about after Charles left me. The house held me together until I knew I was whole again within myself. But now we are both crippled. My atmosphere in the house is already disintegrating. Someone else will come along and create a new, a different atmosphere. They will add features, destroy others, change colours and put a different emphasis. My home will be re-invented, become a different place, my influence will be banished forever. Or will minute traces remain? For myself no such renovation is possible. I can only hold on to the wholeness within in order to cope with my outward deficiencies.

I wonder what the time is? I seem to have been in bed for ages and I can't sleep. The Vanbruyns were very sweet when they came this evening. I liked their matter of factness. No Latin emotionalism there. Easier for me to cope with at the moment. They say they are coming to London in the spring and will come and see me. So that's something to look forward to. I wish I could get to sleep. I don't seem to be able to sleep much any more. I sort of catnap and then wake up with a start and wonder where I am. A few more days and then we go. It's not just a bad dream from which I will wake up. It's reality. Just as it's reality that I want to pee and can't get out of bed. Should I call Hilary? No, the poor girl has been working so hard I mustn't wake her. Anyway I'm all parcelled up in my night nappies and plastic pants – like a baby. I must just put up with it.

The Move

The move to Bath was now imminent. Faith and Oliver were not yet married, as Faith wanted to get the move over with first. She had felt the need to take one thing at a time, and preparing to sell the house, the home where she and Morgan had raised their children and been happy, left her floundering in a sea of uncertainty and doubt. Was she doing the right thing? Where did her future lie and how would her marriage to Oliver pan out for all of them?

There was nobody to communicate her doubts to, nor did she want to communicate them even supposing there had been someone. Unspoken, doubts do not harden into certainties; once communicated they cannot be stifled. All Faith's friends were pleased at the prospect of her remarriage, they saw it as a 'good thing'. She would be forty-two on her next birthday and decisions put off were very often decisions never taken. She certainly couldn't talk to Jocelyn, who was completely absorbed in her own life as was natural at her age. Bath was where the current boyfriend lived so Bath was OK by her. She could not see beyond this. Faith went ahead and in the busyness of activity her doubts were submerged.

At this moment Faith was sorting out the remnants in Hilary's room. With Hilary in Israel her mother had not wished to throw anything out, although there was plenty of what Faith would call rubbish which she felt should have been destined for the rubbish bin. Faith herself was a great thrower-outer and during the packing process she encouraged her younger daughter not to hoard.

'Life is a process of accumulation and at intervals it helps to shed some of one's personal possessions,' she told her.

But with Hilary's things it was different. She was not there to make the decisions and Faith modified her ruthless discarding mood, cramming everything into boxes for Hilary to sort out when she returned home. The removers were coming tomorrow and much of the stuff, like clothes, would remain in the drawers. It was the odds and ends which Faith was gathering up herself.

She was having difficulty in closing the bottom drawer of Hilary's small bureau, which had once belonged to Faith's mother and, on her death, had been bequeathed to Hilary. Faith had just emptied the entire contents of the drawer into the box which contained Hilary's treasures. She was putting the drawer back and was unable to shut it properly. She pulled it right open again and gave it a smart shove but still it would not close. She then stretched her arm into the back of the bureau and felt something underneath the drawer, obstructing it. She drew out an old school exercise book which had fallen down the back. The drawer then shut perfectly. Faith was about to throw the exercise book into the box along with the rest of the miscellaneous collection, but something moved her to open it. She glanced at the first page, read what was written, turned over several more pages and then laid the somewhat tattered book on the window ledge.

The next day was fine and sunny – perfect for a removal. Faith had slept that night for the last time in her own house, in her own bed.

The bed was not going to Oliver's house but into store until the day one of the girls might have need of it. Jocelyn had been given a choice between two rooms in Oliver's house and the one she had chosen was in the body of the house while the other, a small attic lit only by two skylights and up a narrow stairway, was where Hilary's furniture and belongings would go. Oliver had installed night storage heaters in the house so it was considerably warmer. He had, however, insisted on single beds.

'I'm not a very good sleeper and you would be very disturbed by my tossing and turning,' he had said to Faith.

He had gone out and bought a pair of comfortable and expensive single beds. When Faith first saw them in the bedroom they were placed a good three feet apart with a low table between them and individual lights on the headboards.

'That looks rather unfriendly,' she had said. 'Let's put them together.' Before Oliver could reply she had pulled the table out from between them. 'Give me a hand to shove them together.'

Without commenting Oliver had done as she asked.

'That looks better.' Faith moved the table to the far side. 'I've got a bedside table that will do for this side.' She straightened one of the lights which had got knocked askew.

'All right?'

'Mm.' Oliver nodded and left the room. Since then they hadn't seen each other, as Oliver had gone off to his office and Faith had driven over to her house to finish off packing up, and sleep the night there in order to receive the removers who had promised to arrive early. Oliver had rung her in the evening as he was in the habit of doing if they were not together. He was a great user of the telephone and often seemed more communicative down the telephone wire than when they were in each other's company.

True to their promise, the removers arrived at 8.30

and by midday, after various tea breaks, the van was loaded and ready to move off to Bath. All the furniture that had been in both the girls' rooms would be transposed wholesale to the Bath house, but some of the other furniture was destined for the depository for the time being. At the back of Faith's mind had been the thought that one day they would sell Oliver's house and buy one together – or even build one – and then her furniture could come out of store to create a more even balance between Oliver's rather sombre pieces and her own more varied possessions. For the present she was content that he had made room for those pieces to which she was most attached.

Oliver returned from work just as the removers were being given their last cup of tea before moving off, having delivered the furniture without mishap. 'All over?' he asked as he walked in and glanced briefly at the two alien chairs filling up the hall.

'Yes, it's all over, thank goodness,' Faith replied. 'But now I have to go back and check on the house. Also I'm giving our gardening tools to our neighbours. You know, the Elliots. In fact they have asked me to supper and I shall probably stay the night.'

'Oh. So you won't be moving in until tomorrow?' Was there a touch a sarcasm in Oliver's voice or did Faith imagine it?

'What about Jocelyn?' he added.

'She'll be back from school shortly. She can get her own supper – there's plenty of food – and then she'll have her homework to do.'

'I see. Well ... see you tomorrow then.' Oliver walked off down the passage towards his study at the back of the house.

Feeling vaguely uncomfortable, Faith got into her car and drove off towards Wiltshire. She had planned it like this. She required time to digest the move, and felt the need to be on neutral ground on this particular night when she had abandoned her old home and not yet rooted herself in the new one. Also she wanted to make a last valediction to the past as she turned the chapter and advanced into the future. That morning with the removers, all had been agitated activity and she had left quickly and abruptly in order to arrive at Oliver's house in advance of the removal van.

As she put her key into the door of the empty house she was assailed by an overwhelming surge of sadness. The carpets had been left so her footsteps did not echo, but memories did. Reverberations of happiness, of sadness, of irritations, and even occasional frustrations and boredom, elements of a life, of several lives, and of the hard slog of everyday family existence. She felt the closeness of Morgan and, twinned with this closeness, a resentment that he should have died and by his dying changed radically the tenor of her life.

Faith shook herself out of this mood. Life was for living. Certainly the past came with her but she hoped in digested form, integrated into her continuing present. She took a last look round her old bedroom, went into Hilary's room and noticed the exercise book on the window ledge where she had left it. She picked it up and put it in her bag.

On leaving Faith made sure that the doors were properly locked and the windows securely fastened. The house was already in estate agents' hands and already one tentative offer had been made and then withdrawn. But she hoped eventually to get a good price.

She loaded the garden tools into the boot of her car with the exception of the motor mower. That would have to be collected later by her neighbours. Then she drove the short distance to the Elliots' house.

* * *

Faith lay back on her pillow and stared up at the sloping white ceiling. The bed was comfortable but narrow on account of the smallness of the room where the Elliots put their guests.

It had been an enjoyable, relaxing evening after the turmoil of the day's events. Her last night in the country. Tomorrow rural sounds would have given way to urban ones. Not that Oliver's house was noisy but the traffic hum could be heard at peak periods. It seemed right to have this night in parentheses, as it were. It was giving her a gap to look back at where she had come from and forward to where she was going. It was going to be all right. Adjustments would have to be made by both of them but they were mature people and capable, she thought, of compromise. One phase of her life was now over, another was about to begin. She felt full of hope.

Faith glanced at the bedside table on which lay the exercise book she had extracted from Hilary's desk. She yawned, stretched out her hand to turn off the bedside light, then changed her mind and picked up the exercise book instead. She was in the wrong really. She knew it. Hilary's diary was her own private property and should have gone in the box along with the rest of her clobber. But Faith had long felt the need for a key to her elder daughter's enigmatic temperament and she hoped in the pages of her diary she might find one.

Faith ran her eye over what was written on the inside of the cover, flicked through several pages and saw that the entries were intermittent and not specifically dated. Only the months were indicated and there were gaps in those. As she leafed through it, an entry leaped out from the page and riveted her attention. A hollow thud seemed to land on her solar plexus. She turned back to the beginning and read.

This is my LIFE BOOK where I am going to write about???? My LIFE of course. KEEP OUT! It's private.

<u>*October 1953*</u>
Went to London with Dad for the day. We went by car to Swindon and then by train to Paddington. Joss was going to come with us but she had a sore throat and a temperature and Mum said she had to stay in bed. I was glad. Not glad that she had a sore throat and a temperature, I don't mean that. But I like being on my own with Dad. He took me to the British Museum and we spent most of the time in the Egyptian bit. Ugh, those mummies gave me the creeps. I liked the jewellery. It could have been fun living in those times – that's if you were rich. No fun at all if you were a slave and had to build those whopping great pyramids. Afterwards we went to a little Italian restaurant and had spaghetti. I had an ice cream as well. Dad had red wine. He gave me a little and said don't tell Mum. I like having little secrets with Dad, it's fun. It was just as well Joss wasn't with us cos Dad and me had a serious conversation about God. Joss is too young and she giggles. Her giggling bugs me. Sometimes she makes me giggle too and that makes me madder at her. I wonder what makes Dad not believe in God. He says it's just fear and superstition. He said that early humans felt so small and alone in the world and the wind and the rain and the thunder and the lightening and the hot sun all seemed so powerful and the moon and the stars and the sky such a mystery that they imagined them as gods and so it went on from there. All sorts of different religions came about. So Dad says God is the creation of fear. Dad's clever but so are lots of other people and cleverer than Dad and some of them believe in God so they both can't be right

– or wrong. How did everything start anyway? Mum doesn't talk about it much but I don't think she believes in God either though she's not so definite about it as Dad. Now I come to think of it Mum is not so easy to talk to as Dad. She's always busy doing this and that. I'll tell you later she says but later she's still busy. Dad always seems to make time. If he's doing something he says half a mo or hang on a jiffy and then he pays attention. The other day when Mum and I were washing up, at least I was doing the drying, I asked Mum what fuck meant. She said I'll tell you when you're older. I heard it at school and I know it's a swear word. I don't want to wait until I'm older. I don't like to appear ignorant at school. I think I'll ask Dad. Dad says that what he believes in or doesn't believe in is called atheism and that Mum is something else. I think he said something like aggrostik. I spose like being an aggro because you're not sure what to believe.

Vile day at school. Annie went off with that simpering Caroline. All because I said I thought her hair looked prettier the way she had it before. Then in R.K. Miss Hammond (she smells) ticked me off for asking what I thought was a perfectly intelligent question and she said I shouldn't question the Bible. I said my father told me to question everything and that he was an atheist. It made quite an impression in class. Hammy said that was his misfortune but I think she meant mine, silly old cow. Instead of going home on the bus I went to Dad's office and came home in the car with him.

Annie's gone off Caroline thank goodness. I thought she'd soon get bored with her. I've asked Dad about fuck and he told me what it means – no big deal. I used it in the playground today when it was home time. I was just about to go out of the gate when my case burst open and all my books fell on the wet ground. Was I livid. Mary Peterson was standing by the gate and she looked quite surprised. She always thinks she's the only one who knows words like that and she likes to show off. I said it quite casually – oh fuck – then I picked up my books. Mary looked as if she were about to say something, she half opened her mouth then closed it again. I just looked at her, feeling superior and walked out through the gate.

<u>January 1954</u>
We all went to London today. Mum to do some shopping at Peter Jones and Dad took me and Joss to the Science Museum. Joss shot about making the models work and me and Dad looked at more grown up things. Then we met Mum in a cafe in south Kensington and had tea and cakes. Joss and I had lemonade actually. It was fun but I like going out with Dad on my own best.

<u>March</u>
Mum and Joss are going to stay with Granny for a few days. Poor Granny is very lonely since Grandpa died and Mum says she's not very well. They are going for five days and Joss will miss some school. At her age it's not that important but it will be when she's older.

Mum and Joss have been gone for three days. Last night I had a terrible nightmare. I dreamt I was climbing a steep, rocky cliff at the seaside and when I looked up there was this horrible monster waiting for me at the top, like one of those outer space things and when I looked down there was the raging sea breaking over great black rocks. I couldn't go on and I couldn't go back. I started to scream and I woke myself screaming. I must have woken Dad too because he came into my room and asked what was the matter. I couldn't answer him and I was crying and shaking and I felt cold. He picked me up and carried me into their bed and I snuggled up to Dad and felt safe and fell asleep. When we woke next morning Dad kissed me and cuddled me and asked me what my dream had been *about. At first I couldn't remember, then it came back and I told him. It was only a dream he said and cuddled me some more. Then we got up and had breakfast and he drove me to school on his way to the office.*

Mum phoned today to say that they were going to stay over the weekend and come home Sunday evening. Gran is very frail and Mum is arranging for someone to come in every day. Hope me and Dad do something special at the weekend.

Didn't do much actually. Dad was busy in the garden and I helped a bit. Last night we watched a spooky film on the box. I sat on Dad's knee. He kept his hand between my legs. It was a nice feeling. I liked it and I didn't like it. Felt sort of empty when I went to bed.

Mum and Joss came back this evening. Joss said she was bored most of the time. Dad cooked a nice supper for us all, helped by me. He'd got the Aga going again. This morning when we went down to have breakfast it had gone out for some reason. Dad made tea and toast and as we weren't dressed and it was beastly cold we took it back upstairs to Mum and Dad's bed. As it was Sunday we didn't have to hurry up. I read my book and Dad read the newspaper. Before we got up we snuggled together and Dad let me feel his thing. It felt all cold and clammy and then it did such a funny thing. It started to move about like it was alive and then it shot up like a jack in the box. I thought it was very odd. Dad told me to hold it again. I did and it was all hard. That's what I made you with Dad said. His hand was right between my legs, it was so comfy. I didn't want to get out of bed but Dad told me to go and get dressed. School again tomorrow. I won't tell Annie, or should I?

<u>September 1954</u>
Mum has started her weaving classes again. She makes some

really nice pieces of cloth. Now she's weaving a scarf for me. I've chosen a sort of green and darkish red and Mum's going to design the pattern of the weave. On weaving nights, me, Joss and Dad get our own supper and sometimes we play a game after. Dad always sends Joss to bed at the proper time but he allows me to stay up later than Mum usually does. Sometimes we look at the telly. When Joss has gone to bed I sit on Dad's lap. I like the way he strokes me. He sends me up to my bath about half an hour before Mum gets home. Quite often he comes into the bathroom when I am having my bath and we play a game of – Find the Soap. I sit on it and he tries to get it out from underneath me. Usually I am just in bed when the car turns in at the gate and then I pretend to be asleep.

October
I went to stay with Annie this weekend. Her brothers are big and noisy but we didn't have much to do with them. The two of us went to the cinema on Saturday afternoon. On Sunday morning we all went to church. I thought of saying I didn't go to church but then I thought that might seem rude and anyway I didn't want to hang around by myself. I quite enjoyed it. It was sort of comforting and the singing was nice. I kept losing my place in the prayer book and Annie's brothers looked at me and sniggered. Annie helped me find it. I felt thick. We had a super roast dinner and apple pie with lots of cream. I've never talked with Annie about God.

November
Something rather awful happened yesterday. Mum went to her weaving class as usual. Joss had gone to bed. Dad had just turned the box off. I was sitting on his lap. He had his hand in my knickers. Suddenly the sitting room door opened and Mum came in. I nearly rolled on the floor Dad stood up so quickly. Mum said her class had been cancelled or something.

She was quite cross that I was still up and sent me upstairs. I got into bed without having a bath, in fact I forgot to clean my teeth. I felt ... I don't know what I felt. I think I felt frightened, yes frightened – and unhappy. Mum came in to say goodnight. I didn't want her to kiss me so I pulled the sheet over my head. Dad shouldn't do what he does, it's wrong. He shouldn't do it. He shouldn't do it.

<u>January 1955</u>
It rained all day today and I got soaked walking home from the bus. I had been to Dad's office thinking to come home in the car with him but he wasn't there. His secretary said he had a hospital appointment. He never told me when we went in this morning.

Annie's getting confirmed in April. She says I should too. You can't not believe in God otherwise there wouldn't be any point in anything. Perhaps there isn't any point anyway. I'd have to get baptised, a bit embarassing at my age. I wish they had done it when I was a baby. I think I'll speak to Mum. Dad'd probably just laugh.

I spoke to Mum last night but she wasn't much help. It seems as if her mind was somewhere else. She didn't really pay much attention to what I was saying. I think I'll go and see the Vicar. He's quite young, not some old fogey. I've seen his kids in the village but don't really know them. They're quite a bit younger than Joss. Perhaps I should go to church. It'd be easier to ask him after the service if I could go and see him rather than just barging into the Vicarage. I wish Annie lived nearer then I could go to her church.

Dad's gone into hospital. For tests Mum says. Dad says he'll soon be home, it was nothing much, just his stomach was giving him problems. I'M GLAD HE DOESN'T DO IT ANY MORE.

I screwed up my courage and went to see the Vicar. Felt a bit of a twit. But he was really nice and didn't look a bit shocked when I said my Dad was an atheist and my Mum was that other thing. I can't remember what it's called now. He is not a bit like Hammy thank goodness. He asked me if I had told my parents that I wanted to be baptised. He was sympathetic and I think took the hint that they weren't all that interested anyway.

Dad's out of hospital and gone back to work. He looks thin and not very well. Mum says they found something which may mean he has to have an operation. I told them I was getting baptised and Mum said she would come to the ceremony if I wanted her to. I said it didn't matter and in the end she didn't come because something cropped up. It would have been nice if she had been there. Annie came.

<u>April</u>
I go to church every Sunday now on my bike and I've started confirmation classes. The Vicar is very good about answering my questions. He doesn't shut me up like Hammy. Actually he's rather smashing to look at. I never thought of clergymen as being good looking. I've always pictured them as being shrivelled and elderly. Mum's been a bit ratty recently.

Dad's gone into hospital for an operation. He says he'll be loads better when they've taken out what's bothering him. I'm praying for him to get better soon. I wish him and Mum believed in God and then they could pray too. Perhaps Mum does. I tried talking to Joss the other day about God but she's such a featherbrain. All she said was – how **boring** – and ran off to play with her mates.

<u>December</u>
I haven't written anything in my Life Book for some time.

*Everything is so confusing. Dad is so ill. Mum says he could die. He's got cancer. The first operation was no good and he'll probably have to have another. Sometimes I wonder if it's God's way of stopping him messing about with me. I suppose I could have stopped it but I half liked it though I knew it was wrong, like telling lies. It was a lie really. But he's grown up, he shouldn't have done it. Grown ups are not supposed to do wrong things. I couldn't possibly talk to the Vicar about **that**. I'd be too embarassed. Besides it wouldn't be fair on Dad. It's like the Vicar is his enemy or something, he's on the other side. Mum's out of the question. Annie? I don't think so. She'd be very shocked and mightn't want to be my friend any more. Besides to tell anyone all boils down to being unfair to Dad, especially now. I just have to keep things to myself. I can talk to my Life Book. In a way writing things down is like talking. When I was confirmed Mum came to the church and the Vicar was quite nice to her. The Bishop confirmed us. I didn't really feel any different afterwards. I thought I might. I go to early morning service on my bike so that I can take communion. It's a bit of a drag getting up so early and not much fun when it's raining. It makes me a bit separate from the others. Of course they're still in bed when I leave. When I get back they're usually having breakfast in the kitchen. Sometimes Dad asks – how was church? – and I don't think he's being sarcastic. He doesn't say a lot these days and I think he's often in pain. We don't talk as we used to and we never seem to be alone together. He only goes to the office now and again and I go to school on the bus every day unless Mum happens to be going that way in the car.*

Joss is getting really cheeky. Last weekend she had a friend staying and when I came back from church they were leaning out of Joss's window and chanting – Holy, Holy, Holy – as I cycled up the path. But Mum heard them and she gave Joss a good telling off.

The Journey

Last time I was in the airport I was on my two legs. I was in charge of my life, I got off the plane, walked through passport control and hung around with the other passengers waiting for the luggage to come sidling through the plastic strips at the far end of the carousel. When my case appeared, I lifted it off the moving band, heaved it on to the trolley and made for the exit. In minutes I was in a taxi and on my way home. Now I sit, marginalised in a wheelchair, while Hilary checks us in. The man who is pushing the chair will have to carry me on to the plane. How demeaning.

Maria will have gone home, dried her tears and be getting on with her own life. From time to time she will think of me and we shall exchange cards. Now and again she will tell some acquaintance the sad story of my stroke and enforced departure. And as she recites the details, her eyes will fill with tears which she will hastily brush away with the back of her hand.

'Well that's done.' Hilary comes away from the check-in desk over to where Faith's chair is. 'I've got us a window and a middle seat which will be best as we'll be first on and last off.'

With the airport employee pushing Faith's chair they move over towards the stairs which lead to the departure area.

'How is he going to get me up the stairs?' Faith asks.

'There's a lift, Mother.'

'Oh is there? Fancy, I never noticed it all these years I've been toiling up the stairs. Well not really toiling, I've always gone on the escalator.'

'This time you're going up in style and when we get to Heathrow there'll be one of those electric buggies to take us and the luggage.'

'I've always wanted to ride on one of those!' They both laugh and the man who is pushing Faith's chair looks at them, slightly puzzled. He has not really understood what they have been saying, his English is minimal.

Hilary pushes the button for the lift to descend. Faith looks around at the other passengers wandering about – it's funny what silly conversations we have to cover the awkwardness of the situation, she thinks. The lift arrives, the door slides open and Faith is pushed inside.

'I'll see you at the top,' says Hilary. 'There's not much room.'

The lift door closes and Faith and her escort go up in silence. Faith can't think of anything to say and she thinks he's probably busy with his own thoughts – must be very boring pushing helpless old people about.

The aircraft is taxying towards the runway. In a moment it will turn for take off. Faith is strapped into her window seat. At this moment there is nothing to mark her out from any of the other passengers. Her paralysed leg is stretched out under the seat in front of her. Her other useless limb lies along the arm rest next to Hilary. It will slip of course and have to be put back, but at the moment it looks quite normal.

Faith has never much cared for flying although of necessity she has flown quite regularly. But she feels insecure in the air with that great void beneath. Although she supposes that to die in an air crash would be to know very little about it, she feels that there would inevitably be moments (minutes even) of excruciating panic beforehand and she would prefer not to have a panic-stricken death.

The plane is turning and comes almost to a halt as the engines rev and gather strength for the mighty surge forward down the runway. This particular moment in the pattern of flying Faith likens to a predatory panther gathering itself together before it leaps on its prey. Usually she shuts her eyes at this point and doesn't open them again until she feels the plane well airborne. But today she keeps her gaze fixed out of the window. She sees the ground rush past, that dark red earth, and as the plane rises and lifts higher and higher into the air and takes a wide sweep out over the sea, Faith looks down on the deep blue water flecked with foam. The plane keeps climbing higher and higher until eventually it levels out. Faith thinks, never will I see this sea again.

When they had left the villa in the morning she did not have much time or space to feel sad, what with Maria and Hilary getting her ready for the journey, copious tears streaming down Maria's cheeks, and then before the taxi arrived, Maria's daughters all came to say goodbye and they too burst out crying. The taxi arrived and the driver had difficulty fitting in all the suitcases, one of which was extremely large. Faith was manoeuvred from her wheelchair into the taxi, everyone trying to help, so that she felt like screaming at them all. Then Hilary locked the front door and gave the key to Maria, who would hand it over to the agents. At last the taxi doors were closed, the driver put the car into gear and they moved off, leaving the little quartet of women waving from the front garden, the bougainvillaea making a vivid backdrop.

'Well that's over.' Hilary stretched out her hand and gave her mother's good hand a gentle squeeze. Faith smiled wanly at Hilary, laid her head back and closed her eyes, only opening them again as they approached the airport.

It is only now, flying high above the Mediterranean, as the aircraft makes for the mainland shoreline and the distant mountains beyond, that Faith feels the real impact of departure. It plucks at the memories of other significant leave-takings, merging them all into one single vibrating chord of valediction.

The sea has disappeared from view as a floor of white cloud forms beneath the aircraft, and above the sky is a pale, washed-out blue. Faith thinks of her white villa standing in its garden of cacti, plumbago, bougainvillaea and the fig tree upon which the original For Sale notice had been hung. Its present silence and emptiness seem to be reaching out to her, and she pictures the sea lapping gently against the small quay which stretches out into Pebble Cove. She can feel tears welling into her eyes. *No, no, I mustn't cry. Poor Hilary has enough to cope with, she doesn't need me weeping, into the bargain.* Surreptitiously, with her good hand, Faith smooths away the damp which has collected on her cheeks from her tear-filled eyes.

Now the cabin staff start the lunch round. Managing this takes all Faith's concentration: to eat without dropping anything; to drink without spilling. She achieves it, with discreet help from Hilary.

During the meal, Hilary's neighbour in the aisle seat waxes social. She is a jolly, fat lady whose ever-blonde hair frames an impeccable make-up.

'Been on holiday?'

'Not exactly,' Hilary replies. 'Have you?'

'I've been to stay with my daughter who's married over

there. I enjoy myself but it's always nice to get home. No place like England I always say.'

'No, I suppose not.' Hilary is not really on this wavelength. 'My mother is coming back to live in England after many years.'

'Ah yes.' The fat lady nods and her speculative eye runs over Faith and alights for an instant on the useless arm which is now lying askew. She leans partially across Hilary and says to Faith, 'Best to be among your own, dear, isn't it?'

Faith, who is sensitive to being patronised by strangers in her present state, gives her a stony look and replies, 'So they tell me.'

Hilary smiles sideways at her mother from behind her paper napkin and the fat lady returns to her lunch. Conversation ceases.

In the aftermath of food, Faith feels sleepy and drops off into an uncomfortable doze. When she wakes up they are deep in grey, wispy cloud and rain is pouring down the windows. The plane buckets occasionally but the turbulence is slight. The sensation in Faith's ears tells her that they are descending, and a voice comes over the intercom to announce their imminent landing at Heathrow. As they come out of the low cloud, Faith can see, not very far beneath them, clusters of red brick houses interspersed with patches of green and laced with grey roads filled with moving miniature cars. The rain looks persistent but not torrential.

She closes her eyes and opens them again, fantasising some miraculous transformation: the blue sea, the distant hills, the coruscating light she has left behind. Instead, she sees the wet grey tarmac rising up to meet them, and almost immediately comes the sudden jar of landing, the juddering decrease in speed, followed by the gentle taxying towards the terminal. My last flight, my last landing

– that's no loss. She watches people collect their belongings from the overhead lockers and slowly shuffle off the plane.

Eventually Faith and Hilary, together with their luggage, are being transported nippily along on one of those electric-driven trolleys, overtaking the foot-slogging passengers. After going through passport control and customs, they approach the exit and, following an undignified hoisting, levering and hauling, Faith finds herself in the back of a taxi with Hilary beside her. They drive out into the rain. There is a heavy build-up of traffic and the journey towards north London is slow and tedious. But finally they arrive at the long tree-lined avenue of tall Edwardian houses, now almost without exception converted into flats or maisonettes. Where once there had been front gardens, cars are now parked and sodden autumn leaves lie thick beneath them.

Faith recognises Hilary's house as they pull up and she realises that she can no longer walk up the steps to the front door.

'We'll be with you in one minute,' says Hilary, getting out of the taxi and hurrying up the steps. Scarcely has she touched the doorbell when the door opens and she and Winnie embrace. Hilary disappears inside the house and Winnie comes running down the steps to the taxi

'Oh Faith,' she says, getting into the taxi and hugging her. 'Welcome home.'

Faith looks at Winnie's round, kind face, wreathed in smiles but with eyes suspiciously damp. She clasps Winnie's hand with her active one.

'You've got a terrible old crock on your hands.'

'We'll manage. We're organised, including a brand new, frightfully super wheelchair. Look!'

Faith turns her gaze to where Winnie is pointing and she sees Hilary pushing a wheelchair up the alleyway by the side of the semi-detached house. It certainly looks a lot more streamlined than the second-hand one she has had at home.

Hilary pushes the chair out on to the pavement, alongside the taxi. The taxi driver, who has unloaded the luggage and carried it up the steps, is obviously impatient to be paid and be off. The crippled old woman is not really his concern but he lends a hand to get Faith out of the taxi and into the wheelchair.

'You take Faith into the house,' Hilary says to Winnie, 'while I pay the taxi and get the cases in.'

Suddenly Faith feels unbelievably tired as Winnie trundles her down the side of the house into the garden. She is accustomed to seeing the garden in the spring or early summer and its present damp, bedraggled autumn sadness is something of a let-down. Faith feels foolish that she should have expected it to be as when she last saw it.

But the room they have prepared for her is warm and welcoming. At the door which opens from the house into the garden, the step has been replaced by a ramp and the doorway is just wide enough to take the wheelchair. There are two rooms on either side of the carpeted corridor and Winnie pushes Faith's chair into the one on the left. Towards the front of the house are two more semi-basement rooms and a bathroom. Upstairs, at street level, where Hilary is at present bringing in the suitcases, are a huge sitting room, a large kitchen and a small dining room which is rarely used.

Faith surveys the room into which Winnie has just taken her and she recognises with a little spurt of pleasure familiar pictures on the walls, her bookcase and her desk, all old friends from the home she has left.

'I expect a cup of tea is what you would like,' says Winnie. 'I'll go and make some.'

While Winnie is out of the room, Faith looks around

her. She doesn't dare move the chair yet until she has familiarised herself with its various levers. Certainly it is much more comfortable than the one she had at the villa. All of a sudden she recognises that the room she is in had been Hilary's and Winnies's. A curtained doorway which she knows leads to a bathroom has jogged her memory.

Presently Hilary comes into the room carrying a small suitcase.

'We'll unpack all your most immediate things now and do the rest bit by bit. I've put the other cases in one of the front rooms.'

'Hilary, you and Winnie shouldn't have turned out of your room for me.'

'Why not? It's nothing. It seemed obvious to let you have the room with the connecting bathroom and we've had the door taken off for easier access. It's no hardship for us to walk a few steps down the passage to the other bathroom.'

'It's more practical all round,' announces Winnie, sweeping in with the tea tray. 'Don't give it a moment's thought.'

'Thank you both so much. You're far too good to me.'

'You wait,' says Winnie with a mischievous smile. 'Wait till you've been here a while. We may turn out to be perfectly beastly!' She filled a mug three-quarters full with tea and puts it on the adjustable table which she moves within reach of Faith's right hand.

'You'll find this room nice and sunny, Faith. It gets the morning sun almost until midday. At least that is if we *get* any sun.' Winnie has sat down cross-legged on the floor and is nursing her mug in her two hands.

'I love the early morning sun,' says Faith. 'It was always my favourite time for swimming in the summer, you remember? Mornings when the sea was like silk and we swam along this shaft of light into the rising sun.'

Hilary is putting away the contents of Faith's little suitcase into the built-in wardrobe. When she has finished she picks up her mug of tea and sits down on the straight-backed armchair, It is the only chair in the room apart from the wheelchair and it strikes Faith that the room is quite sparsely furnished. Room for manoeuvre, she thinks. Hilary all but pre-empts this thought when she says, 'We haven't put much furniture in here because we thought it would be best for you to have to negotiate as few obstacles as possible. But if there's anything you really want, just tell us.'

'As long as I have my music and the radio, there's not much else I need. Come to think of it, now I am in England I'll probably be listening quite a lot to Radio 4.'

'You didn't bring your television?' Winnie asks.

'No, I gave it to one of Maria's daughters. It was quite old anyway. I'll probably get another one here. We'll see.'

This day is over. I am in bed and I've just turned out the light. I can hear Hilary and Winnie moving about upstairs. In fact, I think they have the television on. Tomorrow is Saturday, they won't have to go to work.

First nights in new places always seem strange. The shape of this room is unfamiliar, the sounds coming from outside are different. I feel in an alien environment and I will have to become accustomed to it. It's not that it's noisy, in fact it's surprisingly quiet but I miss the *sound* of the silence which enveloped the villa at night. Over there, whatever sounds there were came to me clearly through the silence as a scythe cuts through the grass. The sound of the sea, the cicadas in summer, occasionally the lonely hoot of a distant barn owl from the trees across the road, or perhaps a solitary plane high up in the night sky. But here tonight there is no real silence and no real sound. The noise of cars, not intrusive but very much there, someone has kicked a tin can, probably by accident; cats are squalling, not far away, perhaps in the alleyway. I know that for miles around there are buildings, and still more buildings and street after street filled with motor cars. But what am I complaining about? No, I'm not complaining, only comparing. And anyway my life will be shrinking, more or less, to the parameters of this room. Little beyond will impinge.

This bed is comfortable but narrower than my own bed was. When they took the cover off I saw it wasn't an ordinary bed but a sort of hospital bed. It has various gadgets, you can wind it up or down, all very ingenious. Winnie explained that I could be 'managed' more easily than in an ordinary bed. No doubt they are preparing for my next stroke. Can't say I blame them. Hope it'll be fatal. But I do miss my old familiar bed.

I suppose one thing my life has taught me is to adapt myself to change. I've learnt that nothing in life is certain, little in life is secure. Only birth and death. Everything in between is fluid, influenced as much by factors outside one's control as by individual decisions. How was I to know that Charles would up and leave me? How was I to know that Oliver was a secret homosexual? How was I to know that Morgan ... that Morgan would develop cancer and die?

I look back and see where I've come from and I look ahead and see where I'm going. Not much room for any more fluidity in that direction, only a gradual compression until I am finally snuffed out. The possibility of another stroke is always present and whether it will incapacitate me further or finish me off I have no way of influencing. All I would petition the powers that be, if indeed there *are* powers that be, is that I may hang on to my marbles until the end. The loss of those would be the final ignominy.

I must compose myself for sleep. I can usually sleep which is something to be thankful for. Perhaps I can manage to die like going to sleep. Though I don't actually want to die at the moment. There are still compensations to being alive and what a waste of all these arrangements if I were suddenly to fall off my perch without having benefited from them. How kind dear Winnie is and how lucky I am to have daughters who bother about me.

Hilary, undressed for bed, pauses outside her mother's door. She opens it quietly. The room is dark and filled with the sound of Faith's slightly rasping breathing. She closes the door again and crosses the passage to her own room.

'She's sleeping,' she says to Winnie as she snuggles up to her in bed.

'Poor Faith – it breaks my heart to see her. She was always so full of energy and bounce.'

'It's not all extinguished yet. Will you still love me when I'm old and paralysed and possibly gaga?'

'Oh do shut up! We're only in our forties.'

'I'm nearly out of mine.'

Re-marriage

After spending the night with her neighbours on the day following the move, Faith had returned to Bath in a state of shocked disbelief. In her overnight bag Hilary's diary burned a phantasmal hole. Had she misconstrued it? Had she read into it what was not there? But Faith knew perfectly well that she had not. What had gone on was stated quite clearly. The worst had not happened and Faith felt reasonably sure that it never would have. What *had* happened was bad enough.

Somehow she could not equate it with the man she knew, or thought she knew. He was, she remembered, the most normal of men, although what indeed constituted normality? If she had not read it for herself she would never have believed it. It could of course be fantasy, Hilary's fantasy. But it read too genuinely for that to be a valid assumption. Instantly Faith recalled the night, shortly after Morgan's death, when Hilary had been so distressed, worrying that her father was in hell. And then there had been that other evening when her weaving class was cancelled, and she remembered the slightly strange atmosphere in the house when she got back, and how Hilary had brusquely rejected a goodnight kiss, and Morgan had seemed momentarily distant, ill at ease you might say with hindsight. At the time she had thought little about it but now it took on quite a different significance.

If only I hadn't found out, Faith thought as she drove along the road towards Bath, her driving reactions mechanical, her mind immersed in the disturbing discovery. *Now the past will never seem quite the same again, Morgan has gone and I can never confront him with it.*

Who could she confide in? With whom could she share this capsule of poison and from whom could she expect guidance and support? Oliver was out of the question. Her various women friends? She had almost blurted it out that morning at breakfast after Kate Elliot's husband had left for work, but something inhibited her. Morgan was dead. This was not an ongoing anxiety. It had died with him.

Oh Morgan how could you! You have left behind a desolation that remembered joys cannot blot out.

What should she do about Hilary? Hilary on the threshold of adulthood and far away in Israel. What did she carry within her that might impede her development towards mature womanhood? Suddenly Faith felt an enormous relief that Hilary *was* so far away. She could just imagine her daughter's fury and indignation that her mother had read her private diary.

Hilary was difficult enough to approach on far less delicate issues, so however was Faith going to bring herself to raise the subject anyway? Whatever approach she might use, it would need to be oblique and tentative, for although Hilary might not deny her father's sexual interference she would be most likely to deny the need for any help in coming to terms with it.

The traffic had become denser as she entered the town and Faith paid more attention now to her driving than to her thoughts. In a matter of minutes she was parked outside Oliver's house and she remained transfixed in her seat, unable to move. Then she shook herself out of her trancelike state, got out of the car and picked up her overnight bag from the back seat. As she put her key into the front door and opened it, it came to her, accompanied by a slight sense of surprise, that this was now her house as well as Oliver's – her home and all that implied.

As she expected, nobody was home. Joss was at school and Oliver had gone to his office. She went up to the bedroom, tidy and marginally clinical with the neatly made single beds side by side. Oliver always hung up his clothes and rarely left anything lying around. Faith unpacked the few things out of her bag and left them on the bed. She picked up the tattered exercise book as if it were hot coal. She would have liked to have been able to drop it into an incinerator so that the information it contained would be obliterated and she could pretend that it had never happened. But instead she took it to what was to be Hilary's room when she came back and stuffed it into the cardboard box which contained miscellaneous books and photograph albums. As she closed the door behind her she decided she would not think about it any more, and by not thinking about it, it would go away.

When she had gone down to the kitchen to make herself a coffee, the phone rang. It was Oliver, and as soon as she heard his quiet, measured voice, she was flooded with reassurance. This was what her life was about now, marrying Oliver and striking out afresh. Hilary was all right in her far away kibbutz. Jocelyn knew nothing. Morgan was no more, and that part of her life was in a past which could not be resuscitated.

Yes, everything had gone fine, she'd tied up all the ends. Of course she was coming to have lunch with him. She'd come to the office.

Faith hung up the receiver and as she drank her coffee, she contemplated the fine rain which splattered against the kitchen window from a slate grey sky.

* * *

Faith and Oliver were married a few weeks after Faith had moved in. It was a quiet affair at the Register Office, followed by a small lunch party. About a dozen friends (mostly Faith's) had been invited to a country restaurant just outside the town. Jocelyn had been present at the ceremony but had ducked the luncheon party with the excuse that she was already committed to go to a pop concert with a group of friends. Faith had accepted this as shorthand for Joss saying she would be infinitely bored to have lunch with what to her fifteen-year-old mind she considered to be a group of old fogeys.

A year into her marriage with Oliver, Faith could no longer smother her doubts that something was seriously wrong. But it was a malfunctioning that she couldn't put her finger on. Oliver was not, in one sense, difficult to live with. He was considerate, good-natured and companionable. They went out fairly frequently, to the theatre, to films and concerts, and on the whole their tastes coincided.

His attitude to the girls was friendly but formal, definitely detached. Faith knew that he disapproved of quite a lot of their goings-on but rarely voiced overt criticism. For their part, Hilary and Jocelyn were polite but tended to ignore him. Hilary had returned from Israel about six months after her mother's marriage. She was busy getting herself to university, which appeared likely to be a northern one so she was not going to be around much anyway.

When she came back from her travels, Hilary was very happy to move into the little attic room at the top of the house. There, she spent a lot of time except when she appeared for meals or to watch the news on television. She rarely watched anything else. Faith found her much easier to get on with than before, more relaxed and open in her attitude to others. She and Jocelyn seemed closer and quite often went out together. There was a great turn-out of her belongings as she was settling in. Clothes got sent to jumble sales, books were sold to second-hand bookstalls and plastic bags full of shredded paper were dumped in the rubbish bin. Faith wondered if she had destroyed the diary – she hoped so. She had decided that nothing useful or positive could be gained for either of them if she broached the subject to Hilary of Morgan's behaviour. Nothing other than acute embarrassment was likely to follow from any opening up of this painful knowledge, illicitly acquired by Faith in the first place. Bury it, cancel it out as if it had never been, get on with the business of living.

Hilary eventually went to Leeds to do a degree in sociology. Jocelyn had finished her A-levels but, unsure what to do next, she was living at home and going through a series of ill-paid and dead-end jobs. Wasting her time, Oliver said. It was around this time that Faith began to feel how inadequate her life was.

She was not as yet actively unhappy with Oliver, but she could not rid herself of the sensation that they were communicating across a gulf, or perhaps it would be more apt to put it this way – they were walking delicately along duckboards laid over swampy ground, one false step and they would be floundering in the mire.

Eventually she homed in on the problem and reluctantly acknowledged to herself that it had its roots in the bedroom. Oliver's sexual needs appeared to be minimal and, when expressed, were clinical and abrupt. He was neither a romantic nor a passionate man. Morgan had been both. Faith was aware that adjustments took time, that it was more difficult embarking on a second marriage in one's forties than a first one in one's twenties. You brought to the second all the baggage of what had been going on previously, and the adaptability of youth is not so readily available. But Faith prided herself on being flexible and open, so when she bumped up against the hard edge of Oliver's thought processes she was baffled. Discuss? Yes of course, what do you want to discuss? he had said. His response immediately dried up the fount of her feelings. She knew that so much between a man and a woman is unspoken, so much that words fail to interpret, so she was at a loss how to proceed further. Mostly Morgan had sensed what she was feeling and they never had difficulty in communicating to one another about what might be on their minds. Certainly they had no problems which stemmed from the bedroom.

Increasingly Faith felt her life was unreal. She had the sensation that she was floating along on automatic pilot, that she was not really in charge. She was happiest when she was out of the house, nosing around estate agents to see what was on the market, or when she and Oliver were socialising with friends or at some public entertainment.

The house conversion had been a success and the three flats were now up for sale. Faith was eager to get her hands on something else. Eventually a broken down old farmhouse had come on the market which offered exciting possibilities for renovation, and she involved Oliver in this project.

In general she did the cooking and shopping, although now and again Oliver made a meal. He was a good cook but finicky and needed to have absolutely all the ingredients to hand. Innovative, he was not. Faith thought he seemed more expansive when they were out of the house and in the company of others. But as soon as they returned home each retreated into a self-enclosed capsule or, as far as Faith was concerned, she felt that she was *propelled* rather than that she retreated. She continued to feel a stranger in the house in spite of the fact that she had plenty of her own things around her. Oliver was not open to change. Once she moved a picture of his, which she thought was badly placed. When Oliver came home he put it back where it had been. Although he did not express any anger, she felt his displeasure and when she tried to make a joke of it and jolly him into discussion, he remarked tartly that he thought it was better where it had been originally.

Twice a week someone came in to clean. She was quite an elderly dame and went back to the time of Oliver's mother. Faith thought she cleaned very badly and longed to replace her but Oliver wouldn't hear of it. 'She's worked here for decades and I'm used to her.' Faith succumbed in the hope that the cleaner would want to retire in the not too distant future. She made it quite clear that she regarded Faith as an interloper. Whatever Faith asked her to do she studiously managed to forget.

Oliver often disappeared into his study. Although he had never said so in so many words, Faith always felt that this was his private territory and she was not welcome to intrude upon it. She did not know what he did there, he would just say 'I'm going to my study' and disappear. If she wanted to speak to him while he was in there she always felt constrained to knock on the door before entering. She knew this was absurd but he never told her otherwise. It was a dark little room with a huge desk taking up most of the space and a small filing cabinet.

By the time Faith and Oliver had been married for eighteen months, both daughters had more or less left home. Hilary was enjoying her course in Leeds and when she did come home on vacation she was out a lot, frequently staying overnight with friends. Jocelyn was sharing a flat occupied by friends of both sexes. At first Faith was not at all happy about it and Oliver's comment that it was probably a den of drugs and promiscuity did nothing to reassure her. Jocelyn was now working for an antiques dealer and although the pay was not up to much she really enjoyed the work. She laughed when her mother expressed reservations about the mixed gender living arrangements.

'Come and have supper one evening, Mum. You'll see what a well organised household we are.'

Faith went and was reassured. In fact she compared favourably the lively, friendly atmosphere in the flat with the low-key waves which washed over her own household, and she wished she could transfer some of it.

She tried to convey the mood to Oliver but his only comment was that they were probably all high on hash, or whatever it was they took.

'Come along and see for yourself one evening, Oliver. I'm sure Joss will invite you.'

'Oh they wouldn't want me.' There the matter rested.

It was December and with the winter solstice approaching, the days were getting progressively shorter. This particular day had been raw and grey with intermittent sleet falling. Considerable progress had been made with the farmhouse and Faith had spent the greater part of this dismal winter morning in the warm showrooms of kitchen and bathroom appliance stores, looking at fittings. It was the bit she liked best – the basics completed, she could give rein to her interior design ideas. She had quite a flair and was so interested that she thought she might take a course in interior design.

She had intended to do some Christmas food shopping later, but the town was so crowded and the weather so foul, she decided to go home early instead. Christmas was proving a bit of a headache. Oliver wanted to go away but Faith felt she should be around for the girls.

Hilary anyway would be home for the Christmas break and Jocelyn's household looked like it was going to dissolve over the holiday, so she was more than likely to decide to come home and might well want to bring a friend (or two). So far nothing had been finally decided.

It was comforting to get into the house away from the inclement weather and Faith was about to go to the kitchen to put on the kettle before taking off her coat but something caused her to pause. A voice issuing from Oliver's study. Never had she known Oliver to be at home at this hour. From behind the closed door came his voice, a clear, resonant voice, as distinct as ever and slightly louder than usual. She went a little way down the passage. It had not been her deliberate intention to listen.

Yes, the coast's clear at the moment. The widow has gone to her farm and won't be in until later. There's no point planning anything until after Christmas. We're probably going to have the widow's hippy daughters for the feast. The elder one is not too way out but the younger one lives in a mixed sex squat and I don't need to tell you what goes on there.

Faith tiptoed back to the hall. What on earth was all that about and to whom was he speaking? Several seconds elapsed before she realised that Oliver had been referring to her – the widow. She did not like what she heard and his references to Hilary and Jocelyn enraged her. She heard the study door open and dived into the kitchen. Footsteps never sounded down that carpeted corridor and in the quiet she held her breath and felt her heart thudding against her rib cage. Then came the click of the front door being opened before it slammed shut. Oliver was gone.

A long sustained sigh escaped Faith's slightly parted lips. What if he had come into the kitchen and found her? What indeed? Why, she wondered as she took off her coat, am I behaving in this way? Why, she continued to wonder as she filled the kettle, did I not go out into the hall and say hello to him, tell him I had come home early because it was such a horrible day, ask him casually what brought him home and then give him a kiss? Why? Because of what she had overheard? Partly that, she supposed. But wasn't it also because deep down she knew that Oliver would not wish to be discovered, would, in fact, hate it and thus another brick would be laid in the wall of non-communication which seemed to be growing up between them.

Faith drew comfort from the mug of hot tea as she pondered on all this. How was it that words, which should open doors, which should be the very stuff of dialogue, could instead be the bricks which built the wall higher? Who had he been speaking to about her in such a manner? Faith assumed it must be some woman but there did not seem to be a lot of space in his life for carrying on an affair. Anyway what was she going to do? Confront him that evening over the supper table? It would have been better if she had done so immediately and not remained concealed in the kitchen. But by nature she was not confrontational.

In the event, the evening passed peaceably. Faith told Oliver about the equipment she had ordered that morning for the farmhouse and he made one or two suggestions, helpful as they always were. He did the washing up and then they watched the news on the box.

'I'm just going to my study for a little,' he said afterwards and Faith went up to bed to read. She was dozing off when he came to bed. He kissed her chastely on the forehead and turned off the light. Soon Faith heard his steady, loud breathing that was almost a snore but not quite. Sleepiness had vanished and she lay rigid, feeling caught in a trap and not knowing how to release the spring.

As it turned out, Christmas went off reasonably well. The girls were in good form and Jocelyn brought along a rather wan-looking young man who mostly sat cross-legged in front of the Christmas tree and strummed away quietly on his guitar. Oliver seemed to be making an effort to be convivial and Faith was momentarily lulled into the illusion that all was well.

Towards the end of January Oliver announced that he had a job to attend to down in Cornwall which would require him to be away for a couple of nights. He mentioned this one morning when he was in the hall with his hand on the doorknob, about to leave the house for work. Progressively Faith had felt herself becoming more and more withdrawn – or wary, was how she thought of it. Whatever Oliver said she looked for the hidden meaning behind the overt one.

At supper that evening she asked him where he would be staying and he gave her the name of an hotel in Padstow and then went on to elaborate on the job – an old-fashioned hotel with new owners who wanted to modernise. His grey eyes engaged her steady gaze without blinking. It had been on the tip of Faith's tongue to suggest that she accompany him, but she held back because the prospect of two days on her own was not unappealing to her. Besides she knew instinctively that such a suggestion would meet with a blank wall of resistance from Oliver.

'Don't bother to ring me, I'll ring you,' he said as he left on the following day.

An unaccustomed sense of freedom invaded Faith. She realised how much living with Oliver created tension within her; tension she had not been acutely aware of but which now became very apparent to her simply because it was no longer there.

She did not quite know what impelled her to go into his study on the second day she was on her own. In a way she was almost surprised not to find the door locked when she tried it.

Faith looked about her, uncertain what she was doing there. It was a cold little room facing north and the only heating was a small one-bar electric fire. She sat down at the big desk, bare save for an Anglepoise lamp, a huge, very clean blotter and the phone, an extension of the main phone which was in the hall. Aimlessly she slid a drawer open and surveyed the contents. They were unremarkable; paper clips, rubber bands, well-sharpened pencils, dividers, a ruler. The next drawer was full of graph paper. She got up and looked out of the window which faced on to the brick wall of the alleyway. Then she turned around and faced the three-drawer filing cabinet which stood in the corner to the left of the desk. She tried all three drawers but the cabinet was locked. She looked in the desk drawers again but could see no sign of a key. Probably, she thought, he's taken it with him. Finally, she opened once again the drawer with the graph paper. She lifted this out and there underneath was a key. It opened the filing cabinet.

Faith hesitated. Should she just lock it up again and leave Oliver's study unexamined? It would have been the more prudent course perhaps but having got thus far she felt compelled to continue.

The top drawer slid smoothly open. It was full of magazines, all neatly stacked. As Faith riffled through them, a crescendo of distaste engulfed her as the realisation of what she had got herself into began to penetrate. She took out the front magazine from the drawer and laid it on the desk where she could turn the pages and really see what it was about.

She had never been exposed to homo-pornographic publications nor, for that matter, to any pornographic material. She knew it was available from certain outlets but it had no relevance for her and this was the first time she had examined it for herself. But her recoil from it was overshadowed by the implications all this had for her relationship with Oliver and their joint future. She felt her bloodstream was congealing in her veins, she had gone so cold. As she returned the magazine to its place and closed the drawer she found her hands were trembling. The second drawer contained more of the same with the addition of a series of exquisitely fine engravings depicting the use of a soldier – apparently from a Scottish regiment – by two officers to satisfy their sexual appetites. The contrast between the delicacy of the execution of these engravings and the coarseness of their content made their impact particularly repugnant. When she opened the bottom drawer she found it empty except for two crumpled, stiffened, white handkerchiefs and she didn't need to examine those to know what they had been used for.

Slowly she turned the key in the filing cabinet lock and put it back where she had found it, replacing the graph paper. She sat down in the desk chair, immoveable as a statue as she stared straight in front of her. Then the phone rang.

The sharp peremptory trill by her elbow startled her and for a moment she was unaware of what it was. Then she lifted the receiver and sent a faint hullo travelling down the line.

'Faith? Is that you, Faith? You sound very far away. Are you all right? It's me ... Oliver.'

'I ... I'm fine. Why have you rung?'

'You don't sound very pleased to hear from me. I'm just ringing to suggest that we go to the theatre tonight when I get back. I'm just about to leave now. You could ring and book the tickets and we'll collect them before the performance.'

'All right.'

'Are you sure you're OK? You sound a bit funny.'
'Yes. Yes, see you this evening then. Bye now.'

Faith replaced the receiver very slowly, as if it were fragile and might break. The theatre tonight. Bizarre, how utterly bizarre. She put her elbows on the desk and dropped her head into her hands.

Flight

When Oliver returned from Cornwall, Faith nursed the expectation that there would be a sudden and dramatic deterioration in their relationship. But life, of course, just carried on as usual. Faith had booked the theatre tickets as requested and, to all outward appearances, they spent an enjoyable evening together on his return.

It was this blanket of normality enveloping them both which muffled the anomaly of their life together. Faith longed to tear it away and at the same time was frightened of doing so. How could she face Oliver with what she had discovered – admit to having invaded his privacy? Admit to having invaded his privacy as indeed she had invaded the childhood privacy of her daughter. Look at what both these excursions into proscribed territory had brought her! Unwelcome and unlooked for information. Information which, in both instances, she did not know what to do with.

Oliver, who was usually even-tempered and considerate towards her had, if anything, become even more affable. If only they could have a row about something, a really big row which would enable Faith to feel justified in hurling her accusations at him. Even so she knew perfectly well that he would simply deny them – flatly and calmly – putting her in the wrong. What solution could she opt for?

One thing she could not now put up with were his, admittedly infrequent, forays into her bed. She made excuses and he retreated without demur. As this all took place after the light had been turned out, neither was truly aware of the other. Several weeks passed and Oliver made no further attempts to make love. Gradually it dawned on Faith that this was just the state of affairs he had probably been aiming for all along. Where should she go from here and how did she handle a situation which appeared only to concern her?

Well before she took the active decision to leave, it lurked at a subconscious level. As the weeks went by the impossibility of her circumstances became increasingly obvious and the possibilities of resolving the dilemma did not increase. She could see no way of approaching Oliver, and yet how could she justify breaking things up when there was no overt sign of dysfunction? Finally she knew she had only two options. She could dismiss what she had uncovered as an aberration which did not concern her and continue with a sexless, companionate marriage which might become more rewarding as they grew older. But she was still relatively young, at least that was how she saw herself.

She had only just had her forty-fifth birthday, surely life had more to offer her than this? Security was not to be bought at any price and anyway she didn't feel secure. How could she, knowing what she knew? She had made one colossal mistake and she had no intention of paying for it. Better to have no bed to lie on than one you have made badly.

Once Faith had taken the conscious decision to leave, she immediately felt better. She felt she had retrieved her life from a void. Her preoccupations were now practical, the nuts and bolts of organisation which she was good at. There was no need to involve the girls until she had actually left. They were not living with her now and were both very involved with their own lives. Talking face to face with Oliver was out of the question, she would leave him a letter and he would have to cope with the situation as best he could. Perhaps he would be relieved, perhaps for him too it had been a mistake. So, when, how and where?

Where to go was what preoccupied her most. She definitely did not want to stay in Bath – the possibility of running into Oliver by chance would always be present. The farmhouse conversion had been most successful and a buyer had turned up almost immediately. With the proceeds from that in her bank account, there was now nothing to keep her in Bath.

Considering various alternatives, she found herself inclining towards London, to the anonymity of the large city. She had never lived in London but was quite familiar with it from excursions made there in Morgan's day with the children. Quite recently a former schoolfriend had taken up an appointment in a London hospital and had moved from Bristol to Chiswick. Like Faith she had two university-age daughters, and had been divorced for five years. She had been urging Faith to visit her in her new home, so Faith took her up on it but without divulging her wider intentions.

Unknowingly Oliver made it easier for her by going off to Wales for a couple of days to oversee work with which his firm was involved. As she packed her suitcases in the empty house Faith had to ask herself whether she was being melodramatic. Oliver's 'see you Wednesday' as he pecked her on the cheek on leaving the house that morning after breakfast, struck a shaft of guilt through her. She felt no animosity towards him, only a sort of loveless neutrality. She had no idea what sort of blow she was inflicting nor how he would react. Would he erupt into anger or anguish, or would he accept her decision coolly and call it quits?

That evening when everything was packed, or at least

everything she intended to take with her for the moment, she sat down to write to him. Writing to Oliver seemed no easier than talking to him, and Faith sat looking at the blank sheet of paper before her and chewed the tips of her fingers for well over half an hour. All that came in to her mind was the most crude message: *I went to your study and saw your magazines and your semen-soaked handkerchiefs and I didn't like what I saw and that's why our marriage can never work and that's why I'm going, goodbye.* But she could not write that to Oliver. He was, in a funny way, too proper. Finally she wrote at length, allusively, hoping he would decode the real meaning of her message but making the point with absolute clarity that her decision to leave him was irrevocable.

Then she put what she had written into a long manila envelope – the only one she could find – and wrote Oliver's name on it. Whereabouts in the house should she leave her communication? Not on the sitting room mantelpiece, that would be too reminiscent of some of the second-class dramas/comedies that they had sat through together at the theatre. Probably the most appropriate place would be on his desk in his study.

Faith went down the passage and turned the handle on the closed door. It resisted her pressure. This time he had indeed locked it. If she had needed anything to stiffen her resolve, the fact of the locked door did it for her. The following morning she propped the letter up against the kettle in the kitchen before she left.

Faith felt slightly lightheaded when the taxi drew up in front of her friend's house in Chiswick. To be uncoupled from one's moorings, even uncomfortable ones, engenders a sense of bobbing about in uncharted waters where the horizon recedes mercilessly further and further. The driver lugged her suitcases to the front door. When it opened, Jane, her friend, let out an exclamation of surprise.

'Good grief, what a lot of luggage! I thought you were only coming for a couple of nights?'

'I know, I'm sorry. I've left Oliver. Don't worry, I'm not landing on you. I didn't want to tell you on the phone. I thought I'd wait till I got here.'

Faith had no intention of imposing herself on Jane. She had embryonic plans for her future and in the meantime intended renting a room or small flat. As things turned out, the two women easily picked up the threads of their intermittent friendship and Jane was insistent that Faith should stay on. Faith was equally insistent that it should be a businesslike arrangement and so it ended up by her paying a modest rent for a good-sized room on the first floor and the two of them sharing the household bills.

On that first evening Faith gave her friend an account of her life since Morgan's death, sketching in the details of her shadowy second marriage. She was not looking for endorsement of her action but she felt doubly vindicated when Jane agreed that she had not had much option. Jane had been through a messy and traumatic divorce from an alcoholic womaniser and was now enjoying her independent life and the return to a full-time career.

In her letter to Oliver, Faith had given him the address to which she was going but no phone number. She was pleased when Jane told her she was ex-directory.

'I did it in order to protect myself from the occasional abusive phone call from Pete when he's pissed.'

Over a week went by and there was no reaction from Oliver. During the day Faith was going around estate agents and inspecting properties that might be ripe for renovation. She came back late one afternoon about ten days after her arrival and when she opened the front door she found a typewritten envelope, postmarked Bath, in the letterbox on the inside of the door. Faith picked it up and went to her room. Jane was not yet home. Had Oliver perhaps gone straight to a solicitor? Was this a solicitor's letter saying he was going to divorce her? Stop pussyfooting about, she told herself – *open* it.

Bath
19.3.1963

My dear Faith

I have tried to make sense of your long, convoluted letter which you say will make it clear why you were left with no other option but to leave me. I can only say that I am as much in the dark as ever I was and am profoundly distressed by your action.

It is very demeaning for a man to be left by his wife for <u>no</u> <u>apparent</u> <u>reason</u>. What do I say to my friends, let alone the butcher, the baker, the candlestick maker, et al? At the moment I am saying nothing except that you have gone on holiday with one of your daughters. This, in the ever present hope that you will re-think your sudden departure and return to Bath.

You make curiously veiled accusations about my having 'other leanings'. I frankly don't know what you're talking about but I always remember Morgan telling me you had a very vivid imagination. The fact that you have 'overheard' (surreptitiously listened to) private phone calls of mine and wildly misinterpreted them, redounds to your discredit rather than mine.

I realise, of course, that as a husband I can never compete with Morgan. I lack his humour, his general joie de vivre and his, I don't doubt, sexual energy. But all that you must have been aware of when you agreed to marry me. Have I in any way treated you badly? Kept you short of money? Been boorish or ill tempered?

If I have failed to behave correctly or shown lack of consideration in any sphere, then please tell me and I will try to rectify it, but don't expect me to make head nor tail of your tangled outburst of innuendo and half truths. What on earth do you mean by 'lack of communication'? We say good morning and good night, we chat amiably about the day's events, both parochial and world wide, we discuss plays and films we have seen together. I may not be as amusing as Morgan but I am every bit as intelligent.

I would have found it more understandable if you had 'gone off' with somebody. But you assure me 'there is no other man'. How am I supposed to react to that? If you are interested, I find it makes your behaviour even more insulting.

We are neither of us in the first flush of youth exactly and I would have thought that you would be glad of the security we can give one another via a civilised companionship. What more can I say? The house seems empty without you and I would beg you to return to your still devoted husband.

Oliver

The letter fluttered down on the bed as Faith tossed it away. A barricade of denial, it left her feeling guilty, in the wrong and hostage to her own sense of impotence.

'After all, what did you expect?' Jane asked her later that evening. 'You knew he'd never admit to anything being wrong. You must just remain firm and sit it out. You don't regret having left him, do you?'

Faith shook her head. No, there was no regret. She

might feel beached at the moment, uncertain of the way ahead – but these feelings were real, substantial. She had brought a tangible reality back into her life, a replacement for that shadowy substance made up of the polite exchange with Oliver which had masqueraded as life.

Oliver's letters came almost weekly and they carried the same message, if differing slightly in the way it was expressed. His bafflement at her action, his social humiliation and – always, always – a plea to rethink and return. No offer of real dialogue and a strong capacity to make her feel guilty. At first she had tried replying, had tried to justify her action but he sidelined any such replies as being 'incomprehensible' and had continued to write as if he were carrying on a monologue, talking to himself, making no attempt to reach out to her and understand what it was she was saying.

Very soon she contacted her daughters, but not before Oliver had already done so and told them that their mother was suffering a nervous breakdown. They both came together to see Faith and were immensely relieved to find her the same as usual.

'I didn't quite believe Oliver,' Hilary said, as Faith made them coffee in Jane's kitchen. 'But still, it was worrying. He said you were staying temporarily with Jane but he indicated that you might need hospital treatment.'

'I'm possibly more in my right mind now than I've been for quite some time. I'm sorry I wasn't able to give you two some prior warning. It all happened quite quickly and I took a fairly sudden decision.'

'Are you never going back to Oliver?' Jocelyn asked, eyeing her mother over the rim of her coffee mug.

'Never.' Faith's reply was vehement in its resolve.

'You don't have to tell us what went wrong,' said Hilary, 'that's your business really. But I always did wonder what made you marry Oliver, he's so different from Dad.'

Faith observed her elder daughter perched on a high stool by the so-called breakfast counter. She saw a confident young woman, soon to take her finals and mature beyond her years. Faith knew how lucky she was as a parent. So many of her friends were having problems with their children; drugs, pregnancies or just plain opting out. She was suffused by a sudden flood of love for the two of them and she knew that if nothing else mattered, they always would. Love is a tide (although its ebb and flow is not so pronounced and regular as the maritime tide) which tugs and thrusts at the emotions keeping them alert and mobile. Faith had always been aware of its movement, both in relation to Morgan and her two daughters. That intermittent ebbing which revealed the flotsam of everyday irritations, minor frustrations, paltry injustices, followed by a renewed flow of love which would wash them all away.

Suddenly it came to her as she sat there drinking coffee with her daughters in Jane's kitchen, that with Oliver there had been no tide, no ebb and flow, only a stagnant opaque pool. With this realisation a sense of lightness entered her being. She felt she had been like a clogged drain now miraculously cleared, which charged her life flow with a fluidity she had not experienced in months.

'Come on,' she said, getting up and putting her mug in the sink. 'It's a lovely day, let's go to Kew.'

In the hall where they were putting on their duffel coats, Jocelyn suddenly flung her arms round Faith.

'I do love you, Mum.'

'And I you.'

'Hey, don't I get a look in on this huddle?' Hilary said, half joking, half serious.

Faith held out her free arm to Hilary and all three had a silent hug before they went out into the spring sunshine.

* * *

Faith's property hunting finished when she decided on an end of terrace house in a street just off the North End Road in Fulham. It was late Victorian and Faith thought it would convert well into two self-contained flats. Fulham was still pretty down at heel, at least in the area where Faith's house was, but distinct signs of better days to come were sprouting. Enquiries at the local council offices revealed council grants for property improvements on quite a generous scale. That, and a survey which was as good as might be expected for such a house, helped to clinch her decision to buy.

Once contracts had been exchanged, Faith decided to move into the house. It was not that she and Jane had any difficulties. In fact her friend tried to persuade her to stay on but Faith needed to feel her independence, needed to embark on a life of her own, on her own. She moved into the top floor of the house. Less work was going to be required upstairs apart from the installation of a kitchen. A square boxroom served for this purpose and once she had the kitchen Faith was quite happy to camp out in the other rooms. She decorated those herself until finally the whole of the top floor was clean and freshly painted.

Meanwhile downstairs she had brought the builders in and from 8.30 to 5.30 the sound of their hammers and drills and non-stop transistor invaded her sound space.

But she didn't mind, she put up plastic sheeting to keep the dust out of her quarters and doled out mugs of tea and coffee when she was around. She was on hand for consultation and just occasionally would shoot off to the builders' merchant when the unexpected lack of some small but vital supply threatened to hold up work for the rest of the day. She became matey with the chaps but not too matey: they knew she didn't look leniently on any slacking off and she wouldn't hesitate to complain to the boss if anything displeased her. The architect put in sporadic appearances but it was not a job of much interest for him.

'I didn't expect to find you living on a building site!' Hilary laughed as she dumped her duffel bag and jacket on the bare floorboards and looked around. It was 6.30 on a Friday evening. The workmen had gone home and Faith was ready to enjoy a noise-free weekend.

'It's a bit of a funny life, I must admit, but there's something quite salutary about living for a while shorn of everything except basic necessities. It's sort of cleansing somehow.'

Hilary wandered to the window and looked out on the street below. Opposite were rather shabby houses, windows shrouded with grubby net curtains. A woman in curlers, a cigarette hanging out of the corner of her mouth, propped up one of the doorways. Hilary watched her remove her cigarette and say something to her black neighbour across the broken-down fence. The other woman nodded her head vigorously and they both looked towards the two small black kids playing in the street. The children paused in their play, looked at one another and with seeming reluctance, one of them kicking a tin can on the way, they returned to their respective houses. The women went inside and shut their street doors. Further down the street Hilary could see another skip in front of a house more radically disembowelled than her mother's. Like the skip in front of Faith's house it was not only full of building rubble, but old tins and bottles as well.

'I won't be living like this forever but it's very practical at the moment. I can keep an eye on the builders and it saves having to pay rent elsewhere. Come into the kitchen and I'll make a bit of supper before we go out to see this film.'

'Wow, you've gone to town here!' Hilary exclaimed. 'It's small but it's wizard.' She sat down on one of the metal-framed chairs with a padded scarlet seat.

'You approve?' Faith opened the fridge to get out the eggs and bacon.

'You bet – very mod-con.'

The kitchen was at the back of the house and looked down on the strip of overgrown garden. On this cool and not very summery May evening, the new leaves on the trees hung limply, scarcely moving in the still air. For the rest, any plants that might be growing were choked under a tangle of weeds and grass. On top of this were bits of wood, stray bricks and plastic cement bags, thrown there by the builders. It was a dismal sight.

'What are you going to do with the back yard?' Hilary asked, having got up from her chair and squeezed past her mother to look out of the window.

'It's a bit depressing at the moment, I know, but once the work is completed, I'll get someone to clear it and rotavate and then I'll see. I want to keep it easy to look after – maybe lay a paved area with tubs for plants. The kitchen in the flat downstairs is going to have sliding glass doors so you can walk straight out.'

Hilary had never taken much interest in her mother's property ventures. This was the first time she had actually looked at anything Faith was doing. She scarcely remembered a time when her mother did not have some project on the go but she never felt it to be any concern of hers. Her most vivid memory of Faith's non-domestic activity was the pieces of cloth she used to bring back from her weaving classes, the scarves and little bags she made for both her daughters.

'Are you going to sell this place when it's finished?'

Hilary took the cutlery from her mother and laid the red Formica table.

'I don't quite know. I might move downstairs and let this one. It's a bigger flat below and there'll be the garden. Or I might sell one flat and live in the other. I don't have to make any decisions as yet.'

'But if you don't sell you won't get any money to do up more properties.'

'True.' Faith put their plates of bacon and eggs on the table and cut some slices from the loaf. 'But I'm not sure how long I want to go on doing this for. I've enrolled for an interior design course and I'm hoping I may be able to earn a living in that area. We'll see.'

'You don't mind living in London?'

'Mind? No, I find it quite stimulating.'

'I've always thought of you as a country person.'

'I love the country but at the moment I think I'm better off in London. Enough talk about me. Tell me how you've been getting on since you got your degree.'

'Not bad. I've been waitressing in Bristol and working in a pub at the weekends to get some money together. I want to go abroad again for a month or two before thinking about serious work.'

'What sort of serious work have you got in mind?'

'Dunno, quite. Thought I might like to train as a librarian. I like books, classification and order.'

'That sounds quite a good idea to go for. I can see you in a library.'

'Mind you I may change my mind, go for something else. It may be a bit static being a librarian.'

'The main thing is you've got a degree under your belt.'

'So have plenty of others.'

'What's our Joss up to these days? I haven't heard from her for a week or two.'

'She's doing pretty well, I think. Her boss is thinking of opening another branch, in Crewkerne I think it is, somewhere like that. He's hinted that when she's had more experience he might make her manager. She seems to have a real flair for antiques. You know she's got a boyfriend?'

'I would have expected it.'

'No, I mean serious – you know, marrying and all that.'

'I sincerely hope not. She's far too young.'

'Don't say I didn't warn you.'

'How about you? Have you got anyone in the offing?'

Hilary wrinkled her nose. 'Too busy really.'

It was raining when they returned from the cinema, that light summer drizzle that scarcely dampens down the dust. The street was quiet and the lamps splintered the raindrops in their beams. When they entered the house their footsteps resounded on the bare wooden stair and their shoes ground gritty dust beneath their feet.

'At least you will have a comfortable bed,' said Faith, 'they're both new. Do you want a hot drink before we go to bed?'

'You don't happen to have a beer, do you? I'm thirsty.'

'I keep a supply for the builders – there's a couple of bottles in the fridge. Maybe I'll join you.'

They sat down at the kitchen table and Faith was thinking what a long time it had been since she and Hilary had been on their own. As she let the cool beer trickle down her throat, she looked at her daughter and then put her thoughts into words.

'Do you still miss Dad a lot?'

Hilary did not answer at once and Faith reflected on how we mourn communally yet each one's grief is private.

'Well, it's over six years now, isn't it, since he died so

it's not so acute. But yes ... I still miss him ... of course I do.'

'You were very close to him. Occasionally I used to say to him that I thought he favoured you over Joss but he always swore he didn't have favourites.'

'I don't think he did. But he and I were great buddies.'

'Too great?'

'What d'you mean?'

Faith could not find the right interpretation and she would have liked to retract her question before she stumbled into too deep water. But there was also a parallel need to shine a light into the dark recess which troubled her. She made an oblique approach, sensing she was treading on wafer-thin ice.

'Do you still keep diaries?'

'Not real ones. Just appointments, dates and that sort of thing. Why do you ask?'

'When I was clearing out the house, just before I moved to Oliver's, I came across an old diary of yours.'

'Oh yes ... and you read it?'

Faith took another gulp of beer and looked away through the bare kitchen window at the lights shining through the trees from the houses at the far end of the garden.

'I leafed through it,' Faith replied, her face still averted.

'Nosey. I wrote a lot of rubbish in my diary.'

'Some of the entries I read about your father ... worried me.' With an effort Faith turned her gaze away from the window and swivelled her head round to look at her daughter. Hilary drained the last of her beer, got up and crossed to the sink where she stood with her back to Faith, meticulously washing up her glass. Silence enshrouded them, a silence Faith found deafening.

Finally Hilary spoke, still twisting the glass under the running tap. 'I told you I wrote a lot of rubbish in my diary.'

'This didn't read like rubbish.'

Hilary turned off the tap, placed the glass on the draining board, then turned round. She leant back against the sink and thrust her hands deep into the pockets of her jeans.

'Mum, Dad is dead. I am an adult. At the moment Oliver is your disaster area which you are in the process of cleaning up. Shall we let the past be, OK? Thanks for the film, I enjoyed it. Now I'm going to bed.'

Hilary bent to kiss her mother goodnight and then, at the kitchen door, she turned and said with emphasis, 'I'm ... all ... right.' She went into the room where she was to sleep and closed the door.

Faith realised that she would never enter any deeper into this episode than she had that night, and perhaps it was a fitting conclusion. Hilary managed her life in a very self-contained way; maybe she was not hostile to help from others but she did not seek it and, in this instance, certainly not from her mother.

After rinsing her glass, Faith turned it upside down and placed it on the draining board beside Hilary's. Then she threw up the bottom half of the sash window, ducked her head and leaned out with her hands on the outside sill. Her glance trickled round the wilderness garden below, an almost full moon gleamed through thin, intermittent cloud. A few ideas of what she might eventually do with the garden crossed her mind. How satisfying were practical problems – they offered solutions. She sniffed in the soft, damp air, it smelled stale and fumy so she withdrew her head and closed the bottom half of the window, opening the top with the new sash cords.

As she lay awake in her comfortable new bed in the bare, scarcely furnished room, Faith experienced a sudden and unexpected implosion of anguish which collapsed the habitual confidence that kept her going. It was as if her entire life force had been drained from her and she lay there, shaking and petrified, the sheet twisted tightly between her clenched hands as if it were a lifeline.

What am I doing here? I must be mad living alone in this half converted house in the middle of Fulham. Oh Morgan ... Morgan, why did you leave me? Your death has raised issues I can't grapple with. I loved you and thought I knew you, but who did I know and ... who were you? There's nothing I'm quite sure about any more. Where can I put my trust? Not in any God, I just don't have that sort of conviction. Look at the mess I'm in with Oliver. It's your fault, Morgan, all your fault.

Faith pulled the sheet up over her head and her body shook in a paroxysm of weeping. Gradually it subsided and she slid effortlessly into the shelter of sleep.

When she awoke the next morning she felt like a convalescent emerging from some debilitating illness, but her mind was clear. Reaching out an arm she switched on the radio. It was tuned to Radio 3 and the full, harmonious music of a Haydn quartet pervaded the small room. She lay there on her back, free of tension, watching the morning sunbeams irradiate the dust particles in the air. Faith often turned to Haydn for solace, she found in his music an order, a gaiety and, above all, an underlying sense of optimism. As she lay listening, she trawled through random thoughts and found last night's panic had subsided.

Her door opened and Hilary, barefoot, padded in with a mug in each hand.

'Mind you don't get splinters, the floors haven't been sanded,' Faith said as she took the proffered mug of tea.

'Don't worry, my soles are like leather. How did you sleep?'

'Fine. And you?' Faith turned down the volume.

'I always sleep well. You're right about that bed, it's

great, really comfortable. What shall we do this morning?' Hilary was sitting on the end of her mother's bed sipping her tea.

'Why not let's go to the Serpentine Gallery, there's an exhibition there I'd like to see. Then if it's nice we could take a boat out for fun.'

'Brilliant. And we'll be almost half way to Paddington. I need to get back to Bristol around teatime.'

It was now several months since Faith had left Oliver. His letters had dried up and although she had a sense of unfinished business, she began to feel that at last it was perhaps safe to allow herself to believe that Oliver had come to accept their separation. So much so, that when the house was finished and she had moved into the downstairs flat, she plucked up courage to ring him, because she wanted to transfer some pieces of her furniture which were in his house to Fulham. He was courteous and unemotional.

'If that's the case you'd better come to Bath to make the arrangements. We could lunch if you would not find that distasteful.'

Faith went to stay with Hilary in Bristol and Oliver met her off the train in Bath on the Saturday. They walked down the platform side by side – two complete strangers. Lunch was frigid – painful silences punctuated by platitudes. The only semblance of animation was introduced by Faith commenting on the technical problems she had come up against with her London property. Oliver made professional comments and then there was a silence again. Faith was unexpectedly overcome by feelings of detached compassion. She would have liked to put her hand over his and say, 'I'm sorry, Oliver.' Of course she did nothing of the sort. When it came to paying the bill, she started to fumble in her handbag but Oliver held up a peremptory hand.

'Perhaps I may be allowed this small favour.'

They went back to his house so that Faith could identify and label the pieces of furniture she had arranged to move to London. She felt phantom-like as she moved around the house sticking self-adhesive labels on her possessions. Nothing had changed; in the bedroom the two beds still stood side by side and as she put the label on the bedside table which belonged to her, it seemed like an act of vandalism.

She came downstairs. Oliver was not in the sitting room nor was he in the kitchen, she looked around and realised that the kitchen was where she had felt most at ease. She remembered one or two kitchen items of hers which she might have liked to remove, but hadn't the heart to do so. She went into the hall and, raising her voice slightly, called to Oliver. He opened his study door and came down the passage towards her. Surely not *that* now, she thought, and then said, 'I've labelled everything, I think. I'll let you know what time the van is coming.'

'Please do, as I'll have to arrange for Mrs Prescott to be here.'

'Thank you for lunch and thank you for letting me come to sort my belongings out.'

'You know that this house is always here for you to return to at any time.'

'Oliver, that's not possible.'

'Goodbye then.' He held out his hand. Faith took it hesitantly. For a moment his eyes held hers and then he moved towards the front door.

'You know,' he said as he opened it, 'I will never divorce you. To me, divorce is the ultimate disgrace, the final admission of failure.' As Faith stepped outside he immediately closed the door behind her.

* * *

Several months had gone by since the Bath visit and the furniture had been safely delivered. Faith had settled into the downstairs flat very happily and was making headway with getting the garden into order. She had not made up her mind whether to sell the property and start again but in the meantime she had enrolled in an interior design course and her imagination was being fired in many directions. The top floor flat she had furnished simply but adequately and had let it on a short-term rental to a young man. His name was Charles Harrison.

Day Centre

I can't quite believe that it is over six months now since I left home. I still think of it as home although my memory is getting fuzzy round the edges and nothing of 'over there' stands out in very sharp focus any more. When the morning sun shines into my room and I see it reflected on the concrete path outside the window, I am reminded of that shaft of sunlight reflected along the smooth silky water in which I used to swim on those still, summer mornings. But much of my old Mediterranean life has become jumbled in my mind.

It didn't take very long to sell the villa and now that it belongs to someone else I'd rather not think about it. But I'm very glad of the money it brought in. I can pay my way and with any luck there will be something for Hilary and Joss if I don't live too long.

It's a funny little life I live now – very compact and predictable. Either Winnie or Hilary brings me a mug of tea first thing and I must say this bed is great, I can put myself upright at the touch of a button. Sometimes one of them brings me my breakfast but if they're pushed for time then it's Susie. Susie is from the Philippines and I'm sure Susie wasn't the name her parents gave her. She's been working for Hilary and Winnie for a long time, cleaning once a week and I remembered her from my previous visits. But now she has given up other jobs to come five mornings a week and mostly she arrives before the others have left for work but occasionally there's a slight gap. She is lively and pretty and very kind to me. She manages the tedious task of getting me up and dressed, not to mention cleaned up, and into my chair with a cheerfulness that is infectious. Although slight she is strong and luckily I am not a heavy person. Once I am in my chair then she tidies my bed before going about the rest of her duties in the flat.

Usually I sit and listen to the morning news on the radio. It's never very cheerful and at times positively horrendous – wars, famines, massacres, corrupt politicians and some in responsible positions who lie through their teeth. Mankind, or should I say humankind? – no, I don't think I will, it's mostly mankind that does not present a very edifying spectacle, it's mainly mankind that does the slaughtering, and womankind and childkind who are the victims.

It's preferable to hear the news on the radio rather than watch it on television. You are spared the visual images – images which are flashed briefly on the screen and which it seems an obscenity to look at from the comfort of a secure home with far too much food in the fridge.

I can hear Susie with the vacuum cleaner down the corridor. She's the one who mostly tries to persuade me to switch on the box – says it's company for me and in a way she's right. Hilary suggested, half jokingly but I think she was more serious than not, that I should get into the Internet – it would open up new worlds for me. I could get coaching to make me literate and then away I'd go, cruising across the ether, clicking on to this and clicking on to that, exploring all sorts of new avenues. Charles and I did have a very simple sort of computer when we had our house agency so it would not be totally strange to me. But I never really took to the computer, although I could see how useful it was for storing information and cutting down on clerical drudgery. I secretly rather liked clerical drudgery, card indexes and all that sort of thing. I sold the computer when Charles left me but I suppose I could get into something more sophisticated if I really tried, say, a laptop. But it would probably be very frustrating trying to use it with only one hand. Besides I don't really want to spend my money on expensive technology nor, come to think of it, have I the slightest desire to explore the Internet. It takes most of my energy just coping on a day to day basis.

Frankly I find all this technology a bit overwhelming. I don't doubt that in the twenty-first century the means of communication will become ever more versatile but I have a nasty feeling that *real* communication between people may diminish, the means interfering with the ends. I'd rather have a letter on the mat any day than an email on my computer.

Basically I am not anti-progress. I just feel all this technology is a bit much. Fine for business but people are allowing it to usurp too much of their private life and it insulates them from what I believe is called the hands-on experience. I mean the sort of things I liked doing when I was able to do them. Activities such as gardening without gloves, chopping wood with my hatchet and sweeping the leaves off the terrace with a straw broom, activities which I felt had atavistic connotations. Who can feel linked to their forebears sitting in front of a flickering screen? And linked we need to be, the present and the future are rooted in the past and we sever this connection at our peril. But then I approve of my articulated bed, my electric-powered wheelchair and I think the telephone the most wondrous invention ever. But again I preferred it when it was *housebound*. Even one of the old men who attends the day centre brings his mobile with him although I swear it's a dummy and he rings pretend numbers just to impress us.

Is that the doorbell? The ambulance – the van, I call it – come to collect me for the day centre? Yes, here comes Susie to help me guide the chair out of the doors and up the side of the house until I reach the pavement. And there's Bill, our driver, all smiles as usual. 'Morning, love' he says without fail every day. Then 'up we goes' as he manoeuvres my chair and me up the ramp. He has a sort of professional patter which he keeps going and which is largely repetitive and without a great deal of thought. But who can blame him, especially as he doesn't get a lot of response from his assorted passengers. You have to laugh really otherwise you would cry. Is this what we disabled elderly have come to at the end of our lives? Carted off to a sort of geriatric playgroup where we have activities in which we may or may not join, according to how cantankerous we may be feeling on any particular day.

I am the only one in the van in a wheelchair, the others are all what the professionals call ambulant, what I call shuffling around under their own steam. Today there are just four of us, it seems that some people don't come every day of the week. There's that little birdlike woman. She's diminutive with a tiny sharp nose and lips pressed together like a sewn-up slit above her chin. She always glares at me from beady eyes that are so brown they appear black. As far as I know I've done nothing to offend her, perhaps she just glares at everyone. Anyway I smile and say good morning but she doesn't make any acknowledgement, just presses her lips more tightly together, if that's possible. And today our mobile phone man is aboard. He gives me a wink and stabs his index finger at his mobile phone which is clamped to his ear and he appears to be speaking into it. Well, when I was a child I had imaginary friends who were totally real to me and I used to think the grown-ups were very stupid not to catch on. So I don't doubt his pretend conversations are every bit as real to him as my friends were to me.

It's Sam however who makes my day. Sam, in a sense, is my mirror image. He is also in a wheelchair but it is his right side which is paralysed and when our chairs are placed side by side we can hold the *Independent* newspaper, which he always brings in with him, between us, and he reads out anything of interest on the left-hand pages and I do likewise on the right. The staff at the day centre think it very funny although actually it's just a practical use of scarce resources. Alone, neither of us could read the paper with any degree of comfort. However we smile dutifully like sycophantic schoolchildren keeping on the right side of teacher whenever the joke about Darby and Joan comes up.

'D-D-Darby and Joan are n-never side by side,' Sam mutters to me as the carer moves elsewhere. 'At least not in the w-w-weather box.'

'Aren't they sometimes when the weather is undecided?'

'I don't think s-s-so.'

I don't know whether Sam's stammer has been caused by his stroke or whether he's always had it. One day I'll ask him. I find it rather endearing. He has the most penetrating blue eyes and very white hair, plenty of it. He's always at the Centre when I arrive, brought in on an earlier transport, probably from a different direction to me. And here he is this morning as usual.

He turns his head and smiles at me as I am pushed into the room. Although his body, like mine, looks slumped in the wheelchair, his expression radiates a vivid alertness which contrasts strangely with the rest of his demeanour. I realise that I am beginning to look forward increasingly to seeing Sam. Certainly my day at the Centre would be inclined to be boring if he were not there, as the rest of our playmates, as Sam calls them, are definitely in the C stream. It's very unkind of me to say that, tomorrow it could well be me. But although they're not really dotty, they're mostly a bit off-centre and communication is limited. True they can move around unaided, but I think I would rather be as I am with my marbles relatively intact. Of course I'm forgetting the blind woman who paints the most wonderful pictures. She's very much all there and seems to know far more about what's going on than we sighted people.

There is a dynamic little person in charge of the art activities here and she's amazing the way she encourages the most reluctant of the elderly potential students to have a go. Of course she's not successful every day with everyone, moods intervene. Some can be led to the water but that may be as far as it goes for that day. I must say, I was a bit diffident myself. But I felt it was ungrateful not to make use of the facilities provided and also I didn't want to be labelled 'difficult'. Since my weaving days I've retained a certain sense of colour and design, but it is difficult to translate this in paint on to paper and my efforts are pretty pathetic, I think. But our instructress takes us all seriously – or she appears to – and is always helpful and encouraging without being patronising.

Sam has always refused point-blank to come to any of the art classes. He is still quite clumsy in the use of his left hand. I feel so lucky to have the use of my right. I suspect that he has always been very good at anything he has done in the past and that it would damage his self-esteem to produce anything less than excellent. Alice has tried very hard to get him to change his mind and although he is always courteous, and marginally flirtatious – Alice is a very attractive young woman – he remains adamant.

'So what m-m-masterpiece have we been working on

this morning?' he asks me when, later on, we are being pushed towards the dining room for our lunch.

'A sort of raspberry-coloured Corot-type landscape,' I say.

'S-s-sounds rather f-frightful.'

'OK, it's not exactly the work of genius but at least I do *go*. I make an effort.'

'In c-c-contrast to me I suppose is what you m-mean?'

'Well you said it, not I.'

At this point we are separated and Sam is wheeled off to a table at the far end of the dining room, while I am placed next to a very large lady with mountains of untidy red hair and whose eating habits do not exactly act as a spur to my appetite.

It took quite a long time before Sam and I talked to one another about our pasts, hung up as we are on our present and the ways in which we deal with it. The minutiae of daily life occupy our attention. There has seemed little time or inclination to delve back into the past or even reveal a more extensive present. And the future? A fast-approaching cul de sac, or could it possibly be an open door?

Our daily life at the Centre is what Sam and I share, the small amusements, the small dramas which frame it. Our lives away from the Centre were an unknown and undiscussed area. I didn't even know whom Sam lived with until quite recently when he happened to mention a son, and then bit by bit he revealed that he lived with his son and daughter-in-law and an adult granddaughter.

'I used to live in Bath before I had this st-stroke,' he tells me one day while we are reading the *Independent* together.

'That's a coincidence,' I say.

'How?'

'I lived in and around Bath when I was young. In fact

I was married briefly to a Bath architect some years after my first husband died.'

'What was his n-n-name?'

'Someone called Oliver Pearson. Why do you ask?'

'I was also an ar-ar-architect. I knew Pearson s-slightly.'

I feel disinclined to go on with this conversation, but Sam is looking at me, turning his head with difficulty.

'So you're the wife who le-le-left him?'

'His only wife, I believe.'

'I never knew much about his private l-l-life. We m-met on two jobs and occasionally I saw him socially at a cl- club we both belonged to.'

'It all seems a very long time ago now,' I say, wishing to close this exchange.

Sam does not press me and we fall into companionable silence. But still my thoughts are not; they dance a jig in my increasingly hazy mind and keep coming back like a tongue to a hole in a tooth – to Oliver, to that bleak marriage and my flight from it.

Resurgent

It never crossed Faith's mind when she let the flat to Charles that he would ever be anything other than her tenant. Quite apart from the fact that he was so much younger, she had only just emerged from the scarring experience with Oliver and nothing was further from her conscious thought than embarking on a new relationship.

She had not communicated with Oliver again since they had met in Bath to arrange for the transfer of her furniture. At long last there was silence. His letters had dried up and he must by now have accepted their separation as final, although he would not contemplate divorce.

Faith was deeply absorbed in her interior design course which fuelled her ambition to become a successful design consultant eventually. She was beginning to enjoy life again and if something was missing she resolutely determined to ignore it.

Charles had told her that he worked in the City but what he actually did Faith had no idea, and little curiosity. To her 'the City' inferred high finance, of which she was ignorant and by which she was bored. He might equally well have been a message boy of course. But he paid his rent promptly and they went their separate ways, meeting occasionally in the hall, when they exchanged everyday platitudes, until that evening their homecoming coincided. Charles asked Faith if she would like to come for a drink.

'Oh I'm too tired to go out again,' she said.

'I didn't mean a drink in the pub, I was inviting you to my pad.'

Faith noted the use of Hilary's word 'pad' and felt even more distanced from him by age.

'Oh well, all right,' she replied somewhat ungraciously. She would much rather have slipped into her own flat and gone into the garden, now cleared of builders' rubble, to inspect the bulbs she had planted in the autumn and which were coming up profusely. But that she could do later and it would seem unfriendly to refuse Charles's invitation. Not that she wished to become friendly – an amicable businesslike relationship was what she envisaged. In fact she wondered as they walked up the stairs to his flat whether he was going to make some complaint, and hoped that a drink might soften her up and make her more amenable to whatever it was he was going to complain about.

But quite to the contrary, he expressed great appreciation of his flat and recounted to Faith all the grotty ones he had previously occupied at inflated rents. He didn't rabbit on about his work, merely confined himself to saying that he was making a nice lot of money at the moment but that the work was all rather boring. Conversely he was curiously persistent in trying to draw Faith out about herself. She was singularly reluctant to give much away and limited herself to saying that her husband had died five years ago and that she had two daughters 'about your age'. This of course was patently untrue, Hilary was probably at least ten years younger than Charles, and Jocelyn more.

When she got back to her flat after this brief social exchange, Faith realised that she did not consider Oliver as a husband despite the fact that they had been (and were still) married. She saw him as a parenthesis, a misplaced parenthesis but one which could not be edited out. Life was not a grammatical arrangement which could be altered at the stroke of a pen or arranged in artificially placed paragraphs. She knew it to be an interlocking chain of events in which choice and fate played equally significant parts. At least that was the conclusion she came to as she washed up her supper dishes in the fading evening light.

She didn't give much thought to Charles. He seemed a pleasant enough young man and she thought she was probably quite lucky to have him as her tenant.

It had been a warm Saturday morning, at the start of one of those rare English heatwaves, in early June. Faith had gone out barefoot into the garden after breakfast to do a little weeding before the sun got too hot. She was squatting down on the brick path and loosening the roots of the weeds with a small fork before actually pulling them up and tossing them into an old shopping basket which she kept for the purpose. She heard the sound of a window being thrown open above her but she didn't look up until a voice called out, 'Good morning!'

She looked up and saw Charles, his torso thrust through the window opening. He leant out with his hands on the window sill.

'What a beautiful morning,' he continued, 'I've just woken up.'

Faith observed the naked top half of his body as she commented that it was going to be a hot day, then found herself wondering whether the unseen part of him was naked as well. With this involuntary speculation she surprised herself and hastily returned her attention to the flower border.

'Have you ever been to Wisley?' Charles's voice wafted down.

'You mean the gardens?' Faith did not look up from her task.

'Yes.'

'No.'

'Would you like to go? It would be a great day for it.'

Faith looked up and lost her balance. When she had righted herself, feeling annoyed by her clumsiness, she sat on the path with her arms clasped around her bent knees. Looking up towards Charles, she saw his elbows were resting on the sill and he was supporting his face in his cupped hands gazing down at her.

'It's a bit of a trek from here on public transport, I haven't a car at the moment.'

'I meant would you like to come with me. I have wheels and I intend going anyway. The weather looks just right for it.'

Faith hesitated. She had no particular plans for the weekend but her instinct was always to say no initially to any proposal she was not absolutely sure about. She searched about as usual for a convincing excuse but nothing came readily to mind and she capitulated with, 'Well, it would be nice to get out of London.'

'Great. I'll be with you in an hour.'

'Make it an hour and a half. I need to go to the shops first.'

'OK.' Charles withdrew from sight and closed the window.

A couple of hours later they were bowling down the A4 in Charles's Triumph Herald, old but solid and quite nippy. Charles had folded back the hood before leaving and the cool breeze combined with the hot overhead sun contrived to make Faith feel pleasantly relaxed. It was of little use trying to talk, most of their words being whisked away on the wind and what remained of them was muffled by the noise of the engine.

Faith sat back in her seat and enjoyed gazing at the floating clouds which drifted across the blue sky above

145

her and at the green fields and copses which sped past on either side. She had never been to Wisley and wondered what brought a young man to these particular gardens, which she had always imagined as the provenance of elderly bespectacled botanists whose eye was on detail rather than floral effect.

'I was brought up with a big garden,' Charles said as they strolled up the path away from the entrance gate. 'During the war my Dad grew lots of vegetables and I used to help him when I was a little kid but the flowers were what I really liked.'

'Do you come here often?'

'No, not really. I've been a member of the RHA for a couple of years now but I can't have been here more than three or four times. It's a real antidote to the City.'

The day was comfortably warm without being blistering, and Faith was suitably impressed by Charles's botanical knowledge which he imparted without being superior or boring about it. She had always enjoyed pottering about in gardens but without any expert knowledge.

When they returned to Fulham in the early evening Faith sniffed with disdain the tired air of the London street as she got out of the car. But she had been refreshed by the outing and felt it would only be civil to ask Charles to supper.

After the Wisley excursion Faith rather lost track of subsequent events. She had practically forgotten what it was like to be wooed; so many years had slithered away since she and Morgan had been young and in love. Oliver's proposal had barely raised her emotional temperature and throughout that disastrous marriage she had remained a discrete entity locked away, as she now saw it, in a sort of emotional autism.

For several weeks she resisted, not so much Charles's passionate persistence, as her own sense that she was about to erupt and overflow like a volcano and that she would be unable to control or guide the subsequent flow of feeling. He was, she told herself, far too young. She had also embarked on that course, to which she had planned to give her undivided attention. What would the girls think, particularly so soon after her debacle with Oliver? She toyed with the idea of giving Charles notice so at least she would not be so aware of his presence. She could feel it penetrating the walls, permeating the ceilings of her rooms; it was just *there*, a felt force in the atmosphere.

She had asked him not to communicate with her for a week or so and he had reluctantly complied, making a joke out of it when by chance they coincided in the hall. He would turn his back on her and say 'I'm not communicating' and then go out of the front door, closing it behind him.

'This is absurd,' he said finally one morning as he sorted the post and handed her two brown envelopes which Faith knew to be bills. 'All I want is to make love to you and it's perfectly obvious that that's what you want as well. So why do you harp on about your age? To hear you talk you would think you were some ancient hag instead of the adorable and desirable woman you are.'

By this time they were out in the street, Faith was hurrying along towards Fulham Broadway station, her head slightly bent against the gusting wind and Charles, exasperated by her urgency, was tripping along marginally in the rear, talking and gesticulating as he walked.

'Just give over, Charles, I'm late and I'm going to miss my train.'

'You're going to miss life if you carry on like this,' Charles retorted.

At the station they parted company, Charles to take an eastbound train and Faith a westbound. She could glimpse him on the platform opposite where he had sat down on a bench and deliberately buried his face in the newspaper to avoid looking across at her. Then he got up as his train approached and raised the now folded newspaper in salute to her before the train came in and obscured him from view.

She knew then that she must succumb.

By the time Charles told her that he had a sailing boat moored in a tiny Mediterranean island port, Faith was impervious to surprises. What had surprised her most had been her own response. She had always regarded herself as a practical, responsible, and 'in-control' sort of person. It was not that during these past weeks she had ceased fundamentally to be any of those things, but they had been submerged under a tidal wave of euphoria. From a prosaic everyday existence, life had taken on a glowing intensity which seemed to block out both past and future, leaving her immersed in a present full of potential and possibility. That perhaps the engine of this vibrant present was the intensive lovemaking they luxuriated in, did not escape Faith. Never had she experienced a comparable degree of sexual activity and it brought her in touch with her essential self as she had not been since Morgan died. After the dreary two years as Oliver's 'wife' (she now always thought of it in inverted commas) which had done nothing for her self-esteem, Charles's warmth, his general enthusiasm for life and his blithe, almost playful affection restored to her that sense of being a woman, a person in her own right and not some shadowy, neutral figure.

'So, you have this boat tucked away in a Mediterranean port? Tell me another.' Faith smiled lazily as she ran her right hand round Charles's chin and then gently tweaked his left earlobe. It was a Sunday morning and there was no hurry to leave the bed.

'No, it's true. I'm not having you on. It belonged to my parents. They were inveterate sailors and returned reluctantly to dry land when the need to earn money arose. After they both died in that car crash I told you about, I went out there and sailed around for several weeks on my own. Having no brothers or sisters to share my grief with, that seemed the most fitting thing to do.'

Charles reached up and brought the palm of Faith's right hand to his lips Then he ran his kisses up the inside of her arm to her armpit. From there on all thoughts of boats, or anything else for that matter, dissolved in the immediate transports of delight which followed.

It was not until later, when they were having breakfast in Faith's kitchen, that Charles reverted to the subject of his boat.

'Why don't we go out there? Have you ever been to the Med?'

'No. The little I've been abroad has been confined to northern and central France.'

'Have you ever been on a boat?'

'A sailing boat? No, I think I'd be terrified.'

'You wouldn't. I'd look after you. I'm a good sailor. I learnt when I was young from my parents.'

'I'm scared of the water.'

'Can't you swim?'

'Yes, just. But I haven't much confidence.'

'You'd soon get it. It's difficult to sink in the Mediterranean, it's so buoyant. And sailing can be so exhilarating, almost as exhilarating as making love.' He picked her hand up from the table and kissed her palm. Absently Faith withdrew it.

'But we can't get away, Charles. I'm on this course, you've got your job.'

'Who said? I can take some leave or I can just leave, full stop. Money's not a problem at the moment and you'd let me off the rent, wouldn't you?'

Faith laughed. 'Hold on, hold on, you're talking as if it has all been decided.'

'Well hasn't it? You can't want to stay in this grey country when the Mediterranean beckons. Go on, just play truant from your course for a week or two. I bet you never played truant from school.'

'No, I did not.'

'Well I did. And it was great fun, roaming about the countryside making my own discoveries instead of being bored in the classroom.'

'Are you bored in your present classroom?'

'Yeah, kind of. Though you make it easier to put up with. But seriously, my love, let's go. It would be a wonderful experience, and what's keeping us here?'

'Charles, go on upstairs and get dressed and leave me to think about this while I wash up the breakfast dishes.'

'Spontaneity is not your middle name, is it?' Charles got up slowly and with obvious reluctance.

'Maybe not. I'm restrained by caution.' Faith gathered the cups and plates together and carried them to the sink. Charles drew his dressing gown round him and tightened the cord.

'Well throw it to the winds then,' he said, kissing her lightly on the cheek before he left to go to his own flat.

What's keeping us here? What's keeping me *here? Nothing that's really important. A few weeks off the course won't really matter. I can always think up some more legitimate excuse than going off to the Mediterranean with my lover. After all I'm paying for the course, no government grants for me. The girls. Well what about the girls? They're absorbed in their own lives. I can't be expected to spend my entire time waiting in the wings in case I'm needed. Mother I may be, but I am also a separate being with my own life. Oh, it would be wonderful, exciting and ... with Charles!*

Faith realised that she had been washing the same saucer over and over again. She smiled to herself as she finished the washing up in seconds.

So, I'm not spontaneous? I'll show him!

They were lying somewhat uneasily at anchor in a small cove between two rocky cliffs. The weather had changed with characteristic Mediterranean suddenness. From blue skies and a light following wind, threatening black clouds had rolled up, the wind had veered to the north and was blowing persistently with every possibility of becoming gale force. Or so Charles feared.

Faith was in the galley concocting something to eat. Charles, on deck, was contemplating their situation and wondering what action he should take. The boat was bobbing about energetically and straining at the anchor. If it didn't hold they could be in deep trouble. He realised they shouldn't have stopped here. He should have continued on to the little port half an hour up the coast. Faith's head popped up through the hatch.

'I've made some scrambled egg. Shall I bring it up?'

'No, I'll come down.' Charles descended to the little saloon where they slept and ate when it was too cool on deck.

It hadn't taken Faith long to cotton on to the fact that life on board was not all that glamorous. She didn't spend much time stretched out on the deck sipping the proverbial G and T. Her hands were reddened and sore from hauling on the anchor chain and she had managed to damage her thumb slinging the fenders out when they entered port. Equally, it hadn't taken her long to adjust.

While Charles had been getting the boat ready for sea they had stayed at a small pension in the port and then he had taken her out for some short day trips just to get her used to things. Two weeks on, she felt she had forgotten all other ways of life. Fulham, her design course, even the girls, all seemed somewhat unreal and whenever she thought about the other aspects of her life, which was not that often, it seemed to her that she was viewing them through the wrong end of a telescope.

She felt increasingly close to Charles and she was intrigued by the fact that he was substantially different on board his boat. He seemed older, perhaps it was the responsibility. There was less banter than on land and he didn't think twice about giving her orders which he expected her to carry out. It was a new experience for Faith to be told what to do, she was so accustomed to being in charge (mainly of herself of course) that she found it quite a refreshing change to be unassertive and drift happily along. Occasionally he shouted when she muffed some vital operation but he never lost his temper. He had tanned quickly and his light brown hair had become blond-bleached by the salt and sun which enhanced the twin pools of his expressive brown eyes.

Now and again anxiety surfaced. The sea seemed so vast and their boat so small, but Charles was at hand to reassure her and he never laughed at her fears. She was still pretty cautious where swimming was concerned but Charles had been right about that Mediterranean buoyancy. Nevertheless, she never swam that far out of reach of the ladder at the boat's stern.

'I think we'll have to move on,' Charles said, stuffing down his scrambled egg at speed and cutting himself a sizeable chunk of cheese.

'Why? I like rocking about in this little bay.'

'Well I think the wind's going to get much stronger and you wouldn't like it if we dragged anchor. We wouldn't be rocking about, most likely we'd be bashing against those rocks.'

'Oh! Do you think it's going to be that bad?'

'It could be and I don't want to risk it.'

'So we've got to put all these sails up again.'

'No, we'll motor.'

And motor they did, hugging the coastline as the sea grew progressively choppier. Dusk was closing in as the promontory came into view with the lighthouse already flashing out its rhythmic signals. It was with feelings of relief that Charles turned the boat landwards and entered the harbour of a small fishing town which he could see was ripe for development. But at the moment it was quiet and empty and they had no difficulty in finding a berth, alongside the quay.

'Perhaps we could do some shopping here tomorrow,' Faith said when they came back from an evening stroll round the harbour. 'We're running low on tins of sardines and that sort of thing and maybe I could find some postcards to send to the girls.'

The departure from London had been precipitate. Once Faith had decided she would go, Charles lost no time in getting them going. Jocelyn, Faith knew, was away in Ireland on holiday. She had tried to get hold of Hilary on the phone but without success so she sent her a very brief note to say that she was going away for a few weeks and not to worry.

How could she justify her carefree attitude to her daughters to whom she frequently preached the value of sober responsibility? They knew nothing whatever about Charles other than that he was her tenant and Jocelyn had one day commented that he was 'rather dishy'. For the first time in her life Faith found herself at a loss to explain her actions. So she felt the simplest course was to dispense with explanation and follow her instincts.

Charles had been correct in his estimation of the weather. Outside the harbour the sea became increasingly turbulent and even in its snug mooring the boat rocked continuously throughout the night, the fenders rubbing against the quay. But when they woke the following morning, not a vestige of the storm remained – a blue, cloudless sky and a sparkling sea greeted them.

After breakfast, which they had in a small bar up some steps and overlooking the harbour, they decided to go for a walk before doing their shopping and setting off again. They were soon out of the town and crossing a small sandy beach, empty at that moment but which on their return contained a smattering of swimmers and sunbathers, forerunners of the tourist hordes which were later to invade it. A rough narrow path led up from the beach to higher ground and it wended its way along the coast, giving wide, clear views out to sea.

'Shall we go on?' Faith asked when they had climbed up to where the path flattened out, slightly widening to become a small dirt road. They could see the distant rocky hills and observe the coastline as far as the headland.

'Why not? Our time is our own.' Charles held out his hand and Faith took it. Mesmerised by the enchantment of the surroundings, invigorated by the sweetness of the air, she walked hand in hand with Charles enveloped in a deep sense of well-being.

She was amazed at what had happened to her. And because somewhere in the deeper recesses of her conscious mind a small voice warned her of the transitory nature of most things, she knew how important it was to live such moments with acute awareness. She had lived long enough for her experience to tell her that nothing lasts except the poetry of the moment and that these moments illuminate the darker passages through which we have to travel. Gently she squeezed Charles's hand and he looked at her and smiled – they walked on in silence for the next five minutes.

'I suppose we *should* be getting back,' said Charles. They had come to a bend in the track and he halted. 'We still have to shop, get the water tank filled up and the fuel tank. We'll be lucky if we get away by midday as we planned.'

'Let's just see what's round the corner.'

Faith had let go of Charles's hand and walked on a few paces.

'Oh look!' she cried, 'what an enchanting spot.'

Charles moved on to where Faith was standing, just round the bend, and looked across to where she pointed. The track continued on for a few yards straight ahead and joined a proper road which led up to the hill town a few kilometres above the port. On the left was a small cluster of quaintly shabby cottages which gave the impression of being fishermen's homes on account of the big double doors. In one of the cottages the doors were open and Faith and Charles glimpsed a boat inside and what looked to be nets draped from the ceiling. A few roughly made steps led down from the dirt track on to a pebbly beach. In front of the cottages was a concreted area with a low wall which presumably protected them from the winter seas.

'Do let's have a look.' Faith was already gingerly descending the uneven steps but Charles, disdaining them, vaulted neatly down from the path onto the beach and held out his hand to help her. They glanced into the open boathouse as they walked past. A man was doing something to his boat, quite a small boat, indeed nothing very large could be housed in such a small space. At the back they observed a rough wooden staircase which must lead up to the two or three rooms on the upper level. They would have liked to get into conversation with the presumed fisherman but lack of adequate language made it impossible. They had to content themselves with an exchange of greeting as they passed by.

At the far end of the row of cottages was a narrow quay jutting out into the cove. They walked out to the end and peered into the limpid water. Shoals of very tiny fish swarmed around the rocks and minute crabs were scuttling up the side of the quay.

Faith straightened up and turned to look at the line of cottages bathed in sunlight which showed up the peeling paint on the doors and upstairs shutters and the poor condition of the whitewashed walls.

'I can't think how we missed this bay when we sailed past last night,' she remarked.

'We were intent on reaching port and anyway it was getting dark,' replied Charles.

Beyond the cottages the ground sloped upwards, an area of land covered in prickly pear cacti with a dominant fig tree in the near corner. Around the base of this land another narrow, rough path wound its way and carried on following the coastline into the distance.

'What's that over there?' Faith asked, screwing up her eyes.

'What's what where?' Charles was looking out to sea and not paying a lot of attention to what was being said.

'There,' Faith pointed. 'There's something hanging on that fig tree.'

Charles turned round. 'I can't see anything.'

'It looks like a notice.'

'Well let's go and have a look.'

They ambled a little way up the path and then clambered up the few feet to where the fig tree grew. A small wooden board was hung on some frayed cord from one of the branches. It looked very weather worn and had nothing on it. But when Charles turned it the other way round, they could both read from faded, red painted lettering what they thought were the words meaning 'For sale'. Underneath was a scarcely decipherable telephone number. It was then that they noticed the piece of ground was badly and incompletely marked out with crumbling breeze blocks.

'No takers, I presume,' said Charles. 'That notice must have been hanging there for years.'

If there was something which in the past had tended to get Faith's adrenaline going, it had been the sight of some broken-down house in need of restoration. Building lots had never played any part in this fever, always there had been some structure to fire her imagination.

'What a wonderful position!' she exclaimed

'Come on, darling. We really must get a move on and get back otherwise we'll never get off today.'

They retraced their steps down the dirt track but before they turned the corner, Faith stopped and looked back again at the little bay with its clustered cottages and the spreading fig tree among the cacti.

Interpreting

I can't seem get Oliver out of my head. Ever since I told Sam the other day that I was married to him, I have this haunted feeling. I wish I'd never mentioned it.

Physically I don't seem to have got much worse since I arrived in London and it's strange really how one can become accustomed, up to a point, to disability, to being crippled. Not an approved word I know, but I'm too old to bother about political correctness so long as I don't upset vulnerable people. But oh dear, my memory! I can't hold anything for very long and I forget who told me what and what it was they told me. But so far I'm not confused about people. I may temporarily mislay their names but I find them again. I know who everybody is, I don't get muddled with people's identities, that would be too awful. But I can see how easily it could happen. Some little connection in the brain fuses and that area is plunged into darkness. I hope I go before that happens to me.

The curious thing is, that when I am actually communicating, I am perfectly intelligent and lucid and know what's being talked about and participate accordingly; when I read a newspaper or listen to the radio, the same applies. Then a few hours on and certainly the next day, most of what I read, heard or spoke about has gone, and it is very rare that I can recall any of it in any intelligible sequence, only disconnected scraps remain. The same is not true when I read a book, that remains in my mind some time after I have read it. Perhaps that's because it has a consistent theme running through it or you are hooked into the characters if it is a novel. I may lose the thread from time to time but if I leaf back a few pages I soon pick it up again. Reading demands concentration and that's what the old find difficult.

Really old age is a shrinking process and disabled old age doubly so. I know I can do nothing about my physical parameters but I fight hard against the shrinkage of my mind and my imagination. Imagination can soar beyond boundaries and bore through physical barriers. If my imagination should shrivel, my whole core would be destroyed.

How lucky I am to be here in this pleasant room, with enough of my own things around me to make me feel connected to what went before and not amputated like you must feel if you were in an old person's home.

But to come back to Oliver, he doesn't often enter into my thoughts and now he may no longer be on this planet why should he invade my mind? I can't remember things very clearly but I know most of it wasn't very pleasant and I'd be happy to consign it to oblivion, which mostly I have been able to do. Morgan intersects my thoughts, like he always has done, but there's something there too that I want to consign to oblivion and I can't now think what it is. It is like having a stone in my shoe, when I walked that is, and it pains me, pains me considerably but I can't remove it. Charles remains like bright sunlight in my mind, and then a black cloud comes over the sun, blotting it out for long periods, but then it always insists on filtering through at intervals. We communicated after he went to the States – that I do remember – but after the birth of his child – silence. I never knew whether it was a boy or a girl and when I wrote I received no reply.

I wonder what time it is? I could put on the light and see. Half past seven. I'd better activate my electronic bed, or whatever they call it, and sit up because soon they will be bringing me my mug of tea. I like to be ready when Hilary or Winnie bring it in so that they don't have to waste their time getting me upright. They work so hard both of them and it must be a great nuisance for them to have me here, but never for a moment do I feel it. Also I don't go on about being a burden because there's not much point in stating the obvious and it's of no help to anyone. Also it's not for ever. Either I shall have a further stroke and they may have to put me in some home or else, and I hope this will be the case, I shall make my final exit.

'Faith, who *are* you talking to?'

I can see Winnie at the door – just. It's dark that end of the room and I always put my bedside light on soft focus first thing in the morning.

'I suppose I must be saying my thoughts out loud although I wasn't aware of it.'

'No harm in that,' says Winnie as she approaches and puts the tea on my bedside table which contains my light, my radio and a couple of books. 'All the best people talk to themselves, I do it myself. It's just that first thing in the morning it's unexpected.'

'That's when my mind, if you can call it a mind, is most active. I come out of sleep refreshed, and everything is quiet and my thoughts roll on rather like those moving walkways in airports.'

Winnie is standing on the other side of my bed now and adjusting my pillows for greater comfort, something I am unable to do.

'There you go, Faith. I must run. I have a rather horrendous day at work before me. See you this evening.' Winnie bestows a quick kiss and leaves me.

I align my useless arm athwart the bedclothes and take the light plastic mug off my side table with my good hand. They've taken to putting a straw in it recently which I suppose makes it easier for me but I don't really care for drinking tea through a straw. Never mind, that's a very minor blip on my life's screen.

I like the early part of the morning. I equate it with a sense of expectancy, of all things being possible. This seemed particularly relevant in that pure, clear Mediterranean light, but even here, though muted, this same sense of expectancy invades me. As I sit up in bed at this moment I am less conscious of my condition and if I could put my paralysed arm out of sight, I could imagine I was whole. I am of course deceiving myself because I want to get up and draw back the curtains. The light is beginning to seep through the fabric and I want to look out into the garden. But I am helpless, I have to wait. That is reality. But there is a dimension beyond reality, beyond the reality of my partial paralysis and that dimension lies in my imagination where I am free to roam unfettered.

Sometimes I think it might be rather nice to be bedridden, I've always had slight Oblomov tendencies. Tucked up cosy and warm with plenty of books and music and a retinue of suitable slaves. Not on, of course, and dangerously foolish of me to contemplate such a thing. Another short circuit in my body and I might well be bedridden but without the capacity to enjoy books or music, let alone be conscious of any retinue of slaves. I would be the slave – slave to my total incapacity. So shut up! Anyway being bedridden would debar me from seeing and talking to Sam.

I am beginning to realise how much I look forward to seeing Sam. Our meetings at the Centre give a focus to my day and I find myself thinking when I read something or hear something on the radio – oh I must talk to Sam about that. Of course I rarely do because it has gone by the time we meet again, unless I manage to make a note of it.

A number of myths are floated about old age I think, expectations of how the old should behave and react. It is not until you reach that labelled enclave that you realise what nonsense most of them are. I suppose there are some people who get taken in by these myths and so, believing in them, they finally become them and in doing so perpetuate them. But each one of us is unique and I would like to hang on to my uniqueness until I die and not allow it to be buried under a carapace of expected attitudes and behaviour. Expected by whom? By the anonymous makers of myth, of course. By conditioned social attitudes. May I die before my uniqueness dies.

'Good morning, Hilary. Thank you for opening the curtains.'

'Not much of a day so far but at least it's not raining.'

Hilary comes and stands at the foot of my bed and I suddenly see in her the rather truculent adolescent, and not the calm woman just recently into her fifties, which she has now become. It's funny really how the child shines through the adult, particularly in parental eyes.

'Joss rang up last night and she wondered whether you would feel up to going to spend a long weekend with her and Mike. She longs to see you and maybe a change of scene would be nice for you.'

A change of scene? It was not something which I had envisaged, or hankered after. Security was what I had with Hilary and Winnie, security and comfort. I thought of Joss's draughty country house, the ever open doors, the barking dogs, the boisterous ... no, the boisterous children were now young adults and most likely wouldn't be there. Of course it would be lovely to be with Jocelyn, but ... Hilary is waiting for my response. How can I be so feeble?

'What a lovely idea. But do you think they will be able to cope with me?'

'Well you won't be as comfortable as you are here. You won't have all your electronic gadgets. But they can borrow a wheelchair and they'll come and fetch you in their big station wagon.'

'And you and Winnie will have a few blessed days of peace on your own.'

'That's not the object of the exercise.'

No, that's not the object of the exercise but it's a useful spin-off. And how they deserve it. It's very selfish of me to feel so hesitant about going.

Hilary moves round to my bedside table and picks up the empty mug. 'So we can speak to Joss this evening and arrange a suitable time?'

'That's fine by me,' I say as I see Susie entering the room with my breakfast tray.

Two hours later I am in my chair, dressed and waiting for the day's proceedings. It's always at this time that I get overtaken by sleepiness, when I'm waiting for the van to arrive. Today is no exception and I try to fight against the drowsiness that invades me. But however hard I try, my eyelids droop and through the French window I see a watery picture of the garden with its concrete path lit by winter sunlight stretching diagonally towards me and flanked on either side by wet grass from which the leaves have now been swept. As I doze off I slip back in time and in my drowsiness I see that sunlit path snaking across the surface of a silky sea on a clear, fresh Mediterranean morning. That sunlit path along which I so loved to swim.

'The ambulance is here.' Susie's soft voice is sufficient to jolt me awake and once out on the pavement, the cold, raw air banishes all somnolence. In the van are all the regulars but there is one missing. The little birdlike woman. I wonder whether she has fallen off her perch.

When we arrive at the Centre I look around anxiously for Sam. He usually arrives before me and – ah yes - there he is in the reception area. He beams his slightly questioning smile across the empty space towards me and I feel a faint fluttering within. No surely not, not at my age, perhaps it was palpitations? One of the carers begins to push me towards him.

'I expect you two want to read the newspaper.'

We are wheeled into a small side room which is more used by staff than – what *are* we? – patients? No, it's not a hospital. Inmates? No, we don't reside here. Customers perhaps, like on the railways where you are no longer a passenger. Clients sounds a bit more upmarket – probably we are just all lumped together as ... oldies.

Whatever, Sam and I are placed side by side and he is unfurling the *Independent* with his left hand. I tilt towards him and with my right hand clutch the pages that are dangling. As I push myself upright the newspaper flattens out, a few judicious shaking movements on both our parts and the crumpled sections are smoothed. It's not an easy operation and we have been known to let all the more interesting pages slither to the floor and be left holding the football results until some kind member of the staff comes to our aid.

Although the door is left open, the everyday noises of the building seem less obtrusive in this little room and we read the paper in comparative quiet. Not a lot of interest today so we intentionally allow most of the pages to slide onto the floor, retaining only the crossword page, which I help Sam to fold so that he can put it on the retractable tray that his chair provides and attempt to fill it in with his not too skilled left hand.

Sam looks around in a way which suggests that he is checking whether or not we are on our own. I say, looks around, but really all he can do is turn his head slightly to the right and even more slightly to the left. But in this cramped movement he manages to convey the greater articulation of which in happier times he would have been capable. Then he says somewhat conspiratorially, 'M-may I ask a rather p-per-personal question?'

'You may ask but you might not get an answer.'

'I'll r-risk that. My question is, was Oliver P-Pearson homosexual?'

I can feel myself close up like a sea anemone. It is unlike Sam to be so direct ... and so personal. I suppose it is a follow-on from the other day's conversation.

I am hesitating in my answer. It is not a question to which a straightforward reply can be given. Sam speaks again.

'I'm s-s-sorry, perhaps I shouldn't have asked such a question. There was always s-s-something about Oliver which puzzled me – I c-couldn't put my finger on it.'

'You didn't know him very well though, did you?'

'We c-c-collaborated on a couple of j-j-jobs and I saw him occasionally s-s-socially.'

'He certainly had problems, sexual problems I mean, and yes, I suppose he was basically homosexual.'

'When we look b-b-back from this p-permissive age, so-called, and realise that when you were married to Oliver Pearson it was a criminal offence to be homosexual! Think of the burden of fear and guilt which weighed on these p-people.'

'Oliver came from a background which was very conventional, very respectable, in the virtuous sense of the word. He was always in complete denial and would discuss nothing. That's what made leaving him the only possible option for me.'

'It must have been a d-dev-devastating experience for you.'

'The focus is very indistinct now. Probably he went

through as much agony as I did if in a different way. I think I suffer from a sort of self-induced amnesia about that period of my life.'

'That's not very s-s-surprising. I hope what followed was happier.'

I am silent. I do not wish to embark on the Mediterranean period of my life, although Sam does now know that I was living there when I had my stroke.

I turn and look at him. I am lucky, I can move my head freely; he is looking straight ahead and his profile is towards me. Up until now I have been aware of the essence of his personality, which shines through his disabilities, but this is the first time I have observed his features with such attention. His slightly receding hairline has increased the height of his forehead, his clear-cut nose just avoids being too big in proportion to his face and the corners of his mouth curve slightly upwards, lending a kindly, humorous expression to his entire countenance. He has a well-shaped head beneath his white close-cut hair and I find myself thinking it is a head I would like to take between my two hands, before I remember that I have only one functioning hand.

Where were you all that time in Bath when our paths never crossed? They might so easily have done, and would my life have been different if they had? All those intersecting lines of communication, missed by a hairsbreadth or fused by chance. I don't think it was palpitations I had when you smiled at me as I arrived this morning, I think it was that perennial spark which is not totally extinguished in me, that spark which ignites the motor of attraction, never mind how inappropriate may be the circumstances.

'You haven't answered my qu-question,' Sam says.

'I have no complaints. It was mixed ... as all my life has been. But Sam, what about you?'

'I was blessed, I don't know why. I was married for

fifty years to the same woman and I never wished it otherwise. She died two years ago from a heart attack and I had my stroke a year later.'

This news pleases me, I like to think of Sam as having had a long, happy marriage. This may well account for his equable, enlightened attitudes. So you wouldn't have had a look-in anyway, I tell myself, thus sweeping all ambiguity out of the way.

Somebody is standing by the door and when I look over I see it is Alice. She raises her pretty eyebrows at me and tilts her head in the direction of the art room. I nod and she comes over and starts to trundle me out of the room.

'I'm off to my art class,' I say to Sam who gives me a quizzical smile and replies, 'Crossword for me.'

Abandoned

It was with reluctance that Faith and Charles returned to London after six weeks on the boat. But it was not before Faith had run to ground the owner of the cacti-covered plot of land by the sea. When they had sailed away that morning after their walk along the coast, Faith couldn't get the picture of that little cluster of cottages out of her mind. She visualised herself and Charles living in a house which changed in shape and size as her mind ranged over the possibilities of the space beside the fig tree.

The owner of the land, who turned out to be an American, was quite surprised when Faith contacted him. Years ago he had bartered his motorbike for the plot. But because other more profitable projects had occupied his time, he had done nothing with it except put it on the market and forgotten about it.

'You wanna *buy* that waste land? OK!' he had said and named a price that was more than reasonable. Of course, the papers were not in order and Faith was going to have to shell out a substantial sum in lawyers' fees to legalise the deeds.

It was the first time Charles had really seen Faith in action and he was momentarily taken aback.

'But, Faith, shouldn't you get a surveyor to take a look before you actually buy it?'

'Whatever for? It's a piece of scrub land, full of stones, with the odd submerged rock, covered in cacti and featuring a rather stunted fig tree. What more could any surveyor tell me?'

'And you think you can build a house on it?'

'I *know* I can build a house on it. It comes with building permission. Up until now I've renovated existing buildings but I've always wanted to build a house from scratch.'

'And then you'll sell it?'

'Sell it? Of course not! We'll come out here to live.'

'Leave England and settle here? Is that what you're suggesting?'

'Why not? What is there to keep either of us in London?'

'What about your daughters?'

'What about them? They've got their own lives, they're more or less adults now. Doesn't it seem like a wonderful idea to leave grey old England and come to live where the light is sparkling and the air pure?'

'Yeah, I suppose so.'

'Whose spontaneity is lacking now?'

Charles had laughed and caught Faith up in a close embrace, then he held her away from him and said:

'I'm not really a stick in the mud, but what do we do about earning a living and all that?'

'I shall continue to renovate houses – we could set up an agency. You've got your City know-how. What about setting up as a financial adviser to rich foreigners or even not-so rich foreigners?'

'I see, you've got it all sussed out, so why should I worry.'

Faith leant her head against his shoulder and looked up at him with lively eyes.

'Exactly.'

Of course nothing worked out in Faith's plan as easily as its conception. There were endless legal complications and she had to make several journeys from England to chivvy the lawyers along. One of her frustrations was her lack of knowledge of the local idiom but she soon got busy on this with classes in London and language tapes. Eventually it all got sorted out and Faith was able to move on to the exciting stage of building the house itself.

She had agreed plans with local builders and they had got started without too much delay. Burt, the American from whom she had bought the land, proved to be quite helpful, introducing her to various local people and now and again acting as interpreter. She had decided that a one-storeyed house would sit better on that particular piece of land and maybe would be finished quicker.

With all that was going on, Faith found little time to pursue her interior design course and finally gave it up. Charles went back to the City and worked hard and saved hard.

Faith was anxious as to how the girls would receive her change of plan. Hilary had been quite cross, and Faith felt understandably so, at her taking off with Charles on his boat.

'You should have told us where you were, Mum.'

'I tried to phone you but you were not available and I *did* send you a note.'

'It wasn't very specific, and what were we supposed to make of your going off on the razzle with your lodger?'

But when it came to the crunch neither daughter put obstacles in her way.

'So long as you know what you are doing,' had been Hilary's faintly disapproving response. Jocelyn had been much more positive.

'Oh Mum, how exciting! You'll be happy, I'm sure you will. We can come and visit, can't we?'

The move itself was quite daunting, in more ways than one and there were moments when Faith was seized with doubts, if not, at times, with actual panic. She had never visualised herself as living outside England. At one level she felt she was making a new start, but then what was a new start? You bring with you, like it or not, the baggage of your previous existence which has to be melded with the 'new' life. Was she being unrealistic in her relationship with Charles, she wondered? She was no longer young but neither was she old, and she knew herself to be a flexible person. She had truly fallen in love with the Mediterranean ambience and felt at home in its environment. In the end it was Charles who silenced these disturbing qualms. After his initial surprise at Faith's plans he became fired with enthusiasm and could hardly wait to get away. He had wanted to marry her but that was not to be. Oliver had refused a divorce when Faith had written to tell him she wanted to re-marry. That brief epistolary contact had disturbed her, but Charles had brushed it all aside.

'Forget it, darling. Marriage doesn't matter.' Faith had felt reassured.

Eventually the move was accomplished. At first the very newness of the house felt constricting and they spent a lot of time moving the furniture around until it felt right. The main feature of the villa, which was modest and even in its very newness did not strike too brash a note, was the big terrace, an extension of the arched veranda, overlooking the sea. Time and again, when they were in the middle of doing some job indoors, they would drift out onto the terrace. As yet there were no chairs so they would lean on the waist-high wall which enclosed it and stare blissfully out to sea. It was late winter, early spring and the air had a wonderful fresh tang, while the sun shone from a clear blue sky. When they had looked their fill they would return indoors, hand in hand, to whatever task it was that they had been performing.

It was on that terrace that Faith was to spend so much time in the ensuing years. From there she would observe the changes in the environment that were to come; there she would think about and have to come to terms with the vicissitudes of her own life.

Their neighbours in the nearby cottages were usually around only at the weekends, They would arrive early in the morning, often before it was light, and if the weather was right the men would go out fishing in their small craft, returning at midday with their catch. Come the summer, the families would move in more or less permanently, the men would go off to whatever jobs they had during the week and the fishing would be a weekend activity. They were friendly neighbours and very soon Faith was able to communicate with them, at least in a basic manner.

Then, as greater affluence gradually seeped in, the cottages were given a facelift; renovation became the order of the day. The boats were put outside or got rid of and the boathouses converted into living rooms and kitchens, running water and bathrooms were installed and ultimately the inevitable TV antennae sprouted from the roofs. But although radically altered within, the cottages preserved their old exteriors, painted and freshened up.

The builders had cleared away a lot of the debris but in common with most builders everywhere they still left rubble lying around. Most of the cacti had been destroyed by the excavations for the foundations and what the builders hadn't uprooted Charles finished off except for the most obstinate. Faith had no love of cacti but for Charles they held a sort of bizarre fascination, so he was quite pleased that some of them had to be left. He worked hard on the land and gradually some sort of informal garden began to take shape. The dry earth, enriched by several sacks of loam, began to proliferate with the light blue of plumbago, the brilliant purple of bougainvillaea and the delicate trumpets of different coloured hibiscus bushes. The terrace was shaded by climbing bignonia once they had constructed the necessary ironwork for it to clamber over. A small tamarisk tree flourished and a variety of succulents served as ground cover and of course that most Mediterranean of bushes, the oleander, filled in several gaps.

Faith would have liked wisteria to grow against the villa wall but it refused to flourish and eventually died. The wizened fig tree responded to regular irrigation and in the course of time they were able to gather figs. By the time a year to eighteen months had passed, the newness had worn off; the villa and its garden had put down roots and could well have been there for decades.

Their life evolved in accordance with their individual and joint activities. Faith sold off one of her London flats, keeping the other as a foothold, as a link with England until such time as she felt she could do without it, which was shortly after Jocelyn got married and Hilary set up house with Winnie.

Once she and Charles had settled in, Faith began to look around for something else she could get her hands on. She found, not too far away, a small rustic semi-ruin. By the time its conversion was completed, the steady influx of tourists had started and there was no difficulty in finding tenants for holiday lets. Which was really the start of their holiday letting business. They acted as agents for various locals who had houses to rent and who were keen to cash in on what was eventually to become a bonanza. Mostly Faith managed the business on her own with just occasional help from Charles.

For his part, Charles had got quite a nice little business going as a financial adviser which gradually expanded and netted an increasing number of clients, so that in the course of time he rented office space in the little port town just up the coast.

Faith blossomed in the combined warmth of the Mediterranean sun and Charles's unvarying affection. Not for years had she felt such inner integration, such a sense of her own personal worth, not since the early days of her marriage to Morgan when the girls had been little. She was happy with a light-heartedness that had nothing to do with frivolity. She felt that her spirit had been purged of the toxins which had entered it since Morgan's death.

Finally she had brought herself to speak to Charles about what she had read in Hilary's diary. At first he was incredulous, inclined to dismiss it as fantasy, but when Faith insisted, he came round to the view that it could be a possibility.

'Even if it was true and you will never know for sure, it's been absorbed into that past which Morgan took with him when he died. It has no place in your present.'

'Of course it has. The past reaches into the present in all sorts of ways. Was I married for all those years to a man I didn't really know?'

Charles shrugged. 'It's debatable. But anyway I don't think we can ever wholly know another human being, no matter how intimate we are or however long we are together. There remains that unknowable core that no other human being can penetrate.'

'Are you trying to tell me something?'

'Only that you must let go of this negative thing that you can do nothing about. Retain what was good about that marriage, and from what you tell me, there was plenty.'

'But maybe it was all illusion.'

'Maybe life is all illusion.'

'Do you really believe that?'

'I'm not quite sure what I believe. All I know is that I'm here with you, that I love you and life is great. Come on, love, let's go for a walk.' He held out his hand, smiling, and reluctantly Faith let him pull her out of the chair.

'I can understand your worry for Hilary,' Charles said as they sauntered along the coastal path. 'But from the little I've seen of her, she seems to me to be a young woman well integrated into her way of life and well able to cope with anything Fate may throw at her. Like her mother,' Charles added with a sideways grin at Faith.

'She doesn't have any boyfriends.'

'Implying what?'

'She may not like men.'

'Meaning she may like women?'

'I don't know. I hope not.'

'Even so there's nothing you can do about that and you can't necessarily link it to what may have happened.'

'No, I know. Hilary has always been very self-contained. She keeps her cards close to her chest, as it were.'

'If you can't alter a situation, then you must come to terms with it, or forget it. Living is about the present, the here and now.'

They were sitting on a huge flat rock down by the sea's edge. Behind them the sun was setting and in front the sea undulated gently; changeless in its changeability.

'Why don't we take the boat out this weekend. It's ages since we've been sailing.' Charles looked questioningly at Faith.

'Let's. That would be lovely.'

When, later on, much, much later on, their life together ended, it was difficult for Faith to separate out those years she spent with Charles. They ran into one another, forming a period of her life in which all currents flowed in relative harmony. That was not to say that the normal frustrations and problems of daily life did not occur, but they were minimal and made little impact. The early passion, which had been the genesis of their Mediterranean life, eventually calmed as was normal, but its spark was always there beneath the surface detonating at intervals to illumine still more the affection of their ongoing relationship. Faith made trips back to England to visit her daughters, and she saw Jocelyn married and came to accept Hilary's ménage with Winnie.

The letting business flourished and it gave her a profitable occupation without making too many demands. When they could spare the time, trips on the boat were a regular activity and Faith grew to love the sea and feel confident in the water. She felt life could not offer her more.

The change, when it came, was so imperceptible as to pass scarcely noticed by Faith. Charles had told her that the volume of his work had increased quite dramatically, and several evenings a week he worked late and said he would have his supper in the port. Now and again he might ring at lunchtime and say he was working through, despite the heat. It was summer. When he came back to the villa, he was often abrupt and uncommunicative. Faith put it down to exhaustion, as she did his sudden abstention from making love to her. By now she was divorced from Oliver and although she had raised the question of marriage with Charles, it had been left hanging in the air.

Then one evening he arrived back unexpectedly early. Faith was sitting on the veranda engrossed in a set of monthly rental accounts. She barely looked up as he crossed the broad terrace and when he sat down opposite to her she greeted him absentmindedly.

'I'll be with you in a minute,' she said without looking up, 'and then we can go for a swim.'

'Faith, I must talk to you.' The desperation in his voice made her look up from the account book.

'And when has that ever been difficult? Just let me finish what I'm doing.' She smiled at him but received no reciprocal response.

'I need to talk to you *now* – this minute.' And he leant across and impatiently snatched the ledger off her lap, tossing it onto the table.

Totally unaccustomed to such behaviour, Faith looked at him in astonishment, which quickly turned to annoyance.

'What on earth's got into you?'

Charles dropped his face into his hands then quickly took them away, got up, and started to pace the terrace.

'I'm sorry, Faith. What I've go to say will hurt you and I don't know how to go about it.'

Faith was about to make some flippant reply about starting at the beginning and going on to the end but when she saw the expression on his face, she checked herself. She remained silent. Charles came and sat down again. He leant forward, his hands on his knees, obsessively plucking his nails against each other. He looked her straight in the face and said, 'Faith, I want to leave you.'

Faith looked at him blankly. She had heard the words, they registered in her brain; even the meaning of those particular words put together in a sentence made sense, but only as words. As a declaration of intent, as an expressed desire, they were meaningless. Charles tried again.

'I know you won't understand this but just recently I've come to feel that my life here isn't enough, I need something more challenging. I can't live this lotus-eater's life for ever.'

'We do *not* lead a lotus-eater's life! We both have businesses to run. We don't sit around in bars getting plastered with bored expats.'

'No, I know. I'm expressing it badly. But I'm not yet fifty, I need to shape up to greater demands. This is marshmallow country.'

'Well, we can always up sticks and go somewhere else. Why should it entail leaving me? I'll come with you.'

'This is what I really have to tell you – I want children.'

'Children that I can't now give you. Who is she?'

'She's American. I met her through Burt. She's quite a bit younger than me. Recently she's been helping me in the office.'

'So, how long has this affair been going on?'

'I've known Ann for four months. I haven't slept with her yet.'

'You expect me to believe that?'

'Not necessarily, but it's the truth. I wanted to tell you first. I'm not a natural dissembler.'

'How very noble of you. So now you can go ahead with a clear conscience. In a nutshell, you want to leave me for a younger woman.'

'Put baldly, I suppose that's what it sounds like but that's not what it is in essence.'

Faith got up from her chair and walked across the terrace. She stood still on the corner and gazed out across the bay. For minutes she remained motionless. Charles did not move from his chair, his gaze rooted on Faith's motionless back. At last she turned round and he could see the restrained trembling of her lips.

'You've stopped loving me?'

Charles stood up and moved towards her. He stopped a few paces from her.

'That I could never do. But Faith, it's different now from what it was. All those discontents I've been feeling, the sense of being understretched, of not fulfilling my potential, of wanting to father children of my own, all those vaguely felt desires only finally crystallised when I met Ann. She was the catalyst, I suppose, that helped me to define things.'

'And you discussed all your feelings with her?'

'Gradually ... yes.'

'Why not with me?'

'How could I? That would have been cruel and pointless.'

'This is hardly kind.'

'I know, but I have to say it.

'We could adopt.'

'No, we couldn't, Faith. That's not what I want and it's not what you want.'

'I want anything that will keep us together.'

'Maybe at the moment. But it would be crumbling cement and give rise to more problems.'

'And this girl is egging you on to leave me.'

'She's fallen in love with me and I'm very very fond of her, but she's not egging me on to do anything. She's sensitive to the situation, she listens but she gives no advice. She waits, but she won't wait forever. You would like her. She's not some mindless blonde bimbo.'

'Pity she isn't, then it wouldn't last. Anyway I'm not into any cosy triangular situation.'

'That's not what I'm suggesting.

'So what then is your plan? You obviously have one.'

'I want to marry Ann, to go to the States and work and raise a family.'

'And all this,' Faith made a vague gesture with her arm, 'means nothing to you? All these years we've spent together?'

'Of course it doesn't mean nothing. It means a very great deal and always will. It's just that I've reached a junction in my life which offers a change of direction and being a selfish bugger I want to follow it.'

'And you want my blessing so that you can go and feel good.'

'I never said that and I certainly don't expect it. Selfish I may be, arrogant I am not. I only hope that one day you may find it in your heart to forgive me for what I'm doing but I know I don't deserve to be forgiven.'

'If I had been young enough to give you children would all this have happened?'

'I doubt it.'

'In the beginning I would have been – just. Why didn't you say?'

'It wasn't an issue then. You had your daughters and our life together was sufficient for my needs then.'

'You could have thought of this before you took up with me. You were the one who was so insistent.'

'And if we hadn't been together, what we would both have missed!'

'And you're prepared to chuck it all away.'

'It will stay with me always. What I want to do now doesn't invalidate what went before. I know there is another course open and plenty of people would tell me it's the one I should take. Stifle all my present frustrations and desires and stay with you, marry you perhaps. And how over the years my resentment would eat away at our relationship, discolouring everything that we originally had until all that was left would be pretence and emotional decay. Do you want that?'

Faith shook her head. She clapped her hand to her mouth but could not stifle the sob. Instinctively Charles took a step towards her and his arms moved marginally from his sides, then they fell back and he turned away. Faith ran off the terrace into the house and Charles heard the bedroom door being closed. For several minutes he stood where he was, irresolute. Then he moved into the house and tapped on the bedroom door. When Faith spoke, her voice was steady.

'Please Charles, go. And don't come back tonight.'

He hesitated a moment and then turned and went out of the front door to the road, where his car was parked. He got in and drove off.

Charles had delivered his bombshell just the week before Faith was due to go to England and she felt that this had been by design. After an initial paroxysm of weeping when she was alone, Faith felt drained of all emotion. She went about on the days before she left like a robot. She knew the die was cast and nothing she could say would influence Charles's decision. He kept out of her way. She had told him to take what things he needed and go to his mistress. Soon to be his wife, she had thought bitterly. He made periodic appearances – they had practical matters to discuss and whenever he saw any small outside job which required doing, he did it as he had always done. Faith made no comment, but she felt a flow of seering sarcasm poised for discharge against him and it was with difficulty that she contained it. The day before she left, Charles came over and asked if he might take her to the airport.

'No thank you. I've ordered a taxi. When you finally leave please give your key to Maria.' She had to look at him with hostile eyes, if not they would have been brimming over.

It had been a relief to reach England, to be away from the emotive scene. When she returned, Charles would have gone to the States, reality would be waiting for her. So far she had told nobody and it was several days after she had been with Jocelyn and Mike that she spoke. The children were finally settled in bed, her son-in-law had gone out to a local meeting, peace and quiet descended. Mother and daughter sat on the lawn under the big oak tree. It was an unusually warm summer's evening. Faith did not beat about the bush.

'Charles is leaving me.'

'Mum, you can't be serious!'

'I'm afraid I am.'

'But why? Why on earth?'

'He's met a younger woman and he says he wants children.'

'But you seemed so happy. You had a great life out there.'

'So it was. But that's what's happened.'

'I thought you seemed a bit subdued this visit. Not your usual buoyant self.'

'I suppose I'll adjust ... eventually. Adjustment seems to be my middle name.'

'The shit! When did you start to suspect?'

'I didn't. He just told me, less than a week ago. Next week he'll be on his way to the States.'

'To *America*? Who is the woman anyway?'

'She's American. She was helping Charles in his office. Charles is going to marry her and will live and work in America.'

'But Mum, what will you do? Will you come back here?'

'To England? No. I've got a life and friends out there. If I have to lose Charles I don't want to lose what is now my home as well.'

By the time Faith got to London to stay with Hilary and Winnie, Jocelyn had phoned them and given them the news. Hilary, a respecter of privacy, was reticent in her comments but quietly sympathetic of her mother's plight. Winnie was her usual affectionate self.

Faith knew that when she returned to her villa, the local grapevine would have spread the story abroad, with or without colourful additions. She was not mistaken. On arrival she was embraced by Maria who promptly burst into floods of tears. Her phone rang frequently. Friends rallied round. Prurient acquaintances masquerading as friends were given short shrift.

Amnesty

Faith is sitting in a wheelchair in Jocelyn's big oak-beamed sitting room. It is a borrowed wheelchair and not so comfortable as the modern one she has in London. She has been with her daughter and her son-in-law for a night and in spite of the rather long and uncomfortable journey yesterday, she has recovered and is enjoying looking through the French windows at the frost-tinged lawn dominated by the big bare oak at its centre.

It had felt strange waking up this morning, not in her usual, familiar surroundings and with the absence of her accustomed routine. Jocelyn had brought her breakfast in bed which, though well intentioned, had not been a very good idea. It had been difficult to get upright on the rather soft mattress and Jocelyn had to enlist the help of her husband. Mike was obviously not comfortable in the role of helper for a stroke-ridden old woman and covered this up with an extra dose of heartiness. He was a golf player and until quite recently also played rugger, so his talk was peppered with sporting allusions. Secretly Faith had often wondered how her daughter put up with him and then she would cover up this thought with that somewhat damning phrase – but then he means well.

Faith had felt like an inanimate sack as her son-in-law heaved her upright. 'There you go, Faith, out of the rough!' His voice was raised several decibels more than necessary. Faith had flinched inwardly.

'Mike, I'm not deaf as well.'

But now Jocelyn has managed to help Faith eat her

breakfast, get dressed and into the wheelchair and has pushed her from the old playroom, where she slept, across the hall and into the sitting room.

Now she sits contentedly watching a persistent robin peck at the frozen ground in hopeful search of a succulent worm, and in the middle distance the curve of the Downs attracts her gaze. She has not experienced such a wide field of vision since she last looked out over that stretch of Mediterranean sea. Her present life is so circumscribed, and the urban vignettes which now and again catch her eye in London as she journeys in the ambulance to and from the day centre, are like snapshots, contact prints which are never blown up. Only when she looks out into Hilary's small town garden does she feel some expansion of her viewpoint.

She feels refreshed by this rural outlook, clothed in the fine transparent mist of a chill winter's day. Though not quite so rural really, as Faith knows from her many visits here in past summers when the hum of the motorway encroaches. But now with closed windows there is only silence and the window-framed landscape.

Jocelyn has come into the room and sits down on an old leather stool close to her mother's chair. She looks up at her with anxious eyes.

'Are you all right, Mum? Is there anything you need? Are you warm enough, would you like a rug to put over you?'

Faith looks down at her daughter and smiles – smiles really at the thought which is crossing her mind – dear Joss, she doesn't change, always wants to do more.

'No thanks, darling, I'm fine. This room is lovely and cosy.'

'We bumped up the central heating because I remember how you often used to feel chilly before, even sometimes in the summer.'

'It's so lovely looking out across to the Downs. I don't get many views in London.'

'Do you hate being in London – obviously I don't mean with Hilary and Winnie – but actually London itself?'

'I'm not that conscious of the environment outside my immediate surroundings. I don't know if you can understand when I say my life is very tight, it's a sort of knot and a lot of my time is taken up with seeing that this knot remains tied, and doesn't come adrift. I have to pay attention to things which before my stroke happened, I wouldn't have given a moment's thought to. It is as if I am a magnet and I have to keep my depleted faculties firmly drawn to me. Like they were iron filings and I mustn't let them get scattered. So of necessity the little enclosure I am in is much more real to me than anything outside it.'

'And what does your enclosure, as you call it, consist of?'

'My room at Hilary's, my very modern wheelchair, the day centre I go to five days a week and the van that takes me there and back. Oh and of course my bed.'

'Is the day centre very boring?'

'No. No actually it isn't. I see other people there, some of them a lot more handicapped than me. I do some painting which is quite fun, even absorbing sometimes.'

'But is there anyone you can really talk to, or are they all fairly cuckoo?'

'No no, not all by any means. As a matter of fact I've made quite a good friend. A very civilised sort of man. We get on rather well, a kindred spirit. He's in much the same state as I'm in. Lives with his son and daughter-in-law.'

'You do make the best of things, don't you, Mum? I'm sure that if ever I have a stroke I shall be impossibly bad tempered and crabbed.'

'Well I hope you won't have one, it's not to be recommended. But like everything that happens in life it helps if you can adapt. Do you remember that game of Scrabble we played when I got the word *fartlek*? Can you recall what it means?'

'Fancy your remembering that, Mum! No, I've completely forgotten its meaning.'

'It's one of the odd things that have stuck in my mind. Plenty more important things I've forgotten. The word's of Swedish origin and is the name for a way of training long-distance runners over varying country and at different speeds. You could say that life was one long-distance run and we're the runners. I expect that's why I remembered it. Not that I'm running now. I need the help of my fellow runners just to keep me upright, metaphorically speaking.'

The telephone has started to ring as Faith is talking. Jocelyn has got up to answer it. It is on the table behind Faith's chair so she cannot see the expression of impatience on her daughter's face as she speaks.

'No, I haven't told her yet. As I said to you, I'm reluctant to. Yes, I know you do. It could cause unnecessary upset. But anyway I will call you back – give me your number again, I seem to have mislaid it.'

Jocelyn replaces the receiver and comes back to where she was sitting. Faith has not paid any attention to the call nor really heard what Jocelyn was saying. Phones have rather moved out of her life though Hilary has offered to get her a mobile.

'Friends or business? If I may be so inquisitive.'

'Neither. Certainly no friend of mine.'

There was something in the tone of Jocelyn's voice which caught Faith's attention.

'No?'

'Mum, there's something been churning over in my

mind and I find it difficult to bring myself to tell you about it.'

'Why?'

'Because it will upset you.'

'You and Mike are getting divorced?'

'Oh God no. Nothing like that. Whatever put that into your head? No, it has to do with you.'

'Then I'd better know about it, hadn't I?'

'I suppose so. That phone call just then was from your Charles.'

'From *Charles*? But from where? He's in the States.'

'At the moment he's in England, not very far away. In Bristol, in fact. He wants to come and see you.'

Faith is silent. She raises her good arm and passes the palm of her hand across her face. Jocelyn continues.

'I was at an auction in Bristol last week and I saw this man looking at me. He seemed vaguely familiar but I meet so many people in the course of my work that I didn't pay much attention. When the auction was finished, I saw him again. He was loitering by the doorway and followed me out into the street. He caught up with me and I heard him say, you're Jocelyn, aren't you? I stopped and looked at him and suddenly realised who it was. Despite the intervening years, and he is considerably changed, I knew unmistakably that he was Charles. I have no very friendly feelings towards him, as you well know, so I kept my distance and was sparing in my comments. But he had a sort of anguished look about him which stopped me from being downright rude.'

'But what is he doing over here?'

'Oh some business trip, I think. And he said something about buying some old English china for friends, that's why he was at the auction. But his priority was to have news of you. When I said you were coming to stay with me he asked if he might see you.'

'And his ... his wife? Is she also over here?'
'No. That was the only personal piece of news he imparted. She died a few years back ... from cancer.'
'Oh no.'
'When he asked if he could see you I didn't really know what to say, I was pretty off-putting. I thought you had enough to contend with. It was no good asking Mike for advice, he's always referred to him since he left you as "that unspeakable bounder" and I doubt if he would want him in the house. In the end I rang Hilary and she said you had a right to know. So here we are, and he's waiting to know from me what you decide.'
'Did you tell him I've had a stroke?'
'Yes, he knows.'

Faith sits silent and Jocelyn waits patiently. She can see this is no easy decision for her mother and wishes it did not have to be made.

'I think ... perhaps ... I would like to see him,' Faith speaks slowly. 'I'd probably regret it if I didn't. But I don't want to upset Mike.'

'I think we can stage-manage that. Mike has a meeting this afternoon at the club house, the golf club that is, he's chairman of the committee. He'll be out for at least three hours, or more by the time they've had a few rounds of drinks. He need never know. I'll ring Charles and get him to come over just after lunch.'

The winter landscape no longer holds Faith's attention, she has retreated into her inner self. Ostensibly nothing has changed. There she still sits looking out of the window, but the landscape is different now. In her mind's eye she sees the little jetty and the blue sea lapping its edges; the sun sparkles on the sea's surface and lights up the turquoise patches where the seabed is sand and not rock.

It is a long time since she has so completely recaptured this image. It is so inextricably bound up with Charles that the discussion of his unexpected reappearance has sent her back in imagination to the place she knows she has never really left.

She cannot be entirely happy with her decision to see him. It has caused a flurry of agitation in her mind which usually is calm and peaceful. All that seems disrupted now and she feels that her decision is not a positive one. It is not so much that she wants to see him but that she doesn't want *not* to see him. That she would always regret.

Jocelyn, who has gone to the other phone to ring Charles, comes back into the room. She turns her mother's chair around, away from the window, and pushes her towards the token log fire.

'He's coming around 2.30. He's got a hired car. It's not difficult to find us. Oh Mum, I hope this won't cause you too much of an upset.'

'Maybe the tying up of a few ends won't be a bad thing. But I could wish that I wasn't as I am. That of course is partly vanity.'

'Your face, Mum, is still lovely, that hasn't been affected at all.'

'Dear Joss, you give me encouragement, but I have to be realistic. The passage of years is bad enough without this other. Also I've got used to being with just my family or others with similar or worse handicaps, so the thought of facing a stranger, who in fact isn't a stranger but belongs to another period of my life, is a bit daunting.'

Later on at lunch, Faith finds herself very tensed up and manages to spill her food, something she rarely does. Jocelyn, sensing her agitation, helps her mother finish the meal by spooning it up for her. Mike keeps his eyes fixed on his plate and shovels in his food at great speed. Not much conversation passes between the three. Finally

Mike gives two suppressed burps and shoves his chair back from the table.

'If you two girls will excuse me, I think I'd best be on my way.'

With Mike's departure the tension lessens, or at least the need to disguise it does. Jocelyn returns Faith in her chair to the sitting room.

'I'm afraid there's not going to be much time for a little nap,' she says, 'but maybe you'd just like to sit quiet while I clear away the lunch things.'

Faith nods as if she is not paying much attention and Jocelyn leaves her to it. Contradictory thoughts twist and turn through her mind.

It is not a good idea, she thinks, to delve back into the past which can never be altered. Only our attitude to that past can change, and perhaps that does then alter what has happened in the past? We can only make sense of the present if we come to terms with what is behind us.

Did I ever come to terms with Charles leaving me? I thought I had, I like to think I have, but the prospect of seeing him again, within possibly the next few minutes, unnerves me. This is absurd. My only reality is the fragile fragment of the present on which I now stand – maybe I should say sit – but which is ever diminishing as my time runs out. This present slithering away to become the past which we can never hold between our hands, only in our thoughts. The future I can observe approaching, implacably. It will keep on coming until, like a film it winds itself off finally on that last particle of our continuing present, be it finite or infinite.

The sharp peal of the door bell causes Faith to start, she has been partially dozing. But now she is totally awake. She hears her daughter go to the door and there is the sound of voices. She wishes she could negate this meeting. Jocelyn has so placed her wheelchair that it is facing the sitting room door so that when it opens she is immediately confronted with Charles. She feels confusion at the sight of this man, at one level so familiar and at another, a total stranger.

Charles comes towards her, followed by Jocelyn. He stops with a certain air of diffidence by her chair and for a few seconds they look at one another, then Faith holds out her good hand towards him. He takes it tentatively, as if it were so fragile it might break, then he places his other hand over the top of it.

'Thank you, Faith, for allowing me to visit you.'

Jocelyn who has been looking at him as if she could quite happily knife him, drags up a chair and says abruptly, 'Sit down.'

She looks at her mother as she says, 'I'll bring some coffee later.' Leaving the room, she closes the door quietly behind her.

Faith looks at Charles and notes his receding hairline although he is barely yet grey. His somewhat rumpled suit gives his body a slackness so different from the taut, tanned body once familiar to her. His face is lined and she can see what Jocelyn meant by 'an anguished look'. But his eyes, those deep brown eyes which so many years ago had melted her and which now hold her own in an unwavering intentness, they have not changed.

'So life has not been exactly kind to you either, Charles.'

'It's been uneven, very uneven.'

'Why did you give up writing to me?'

'For many reasons, Faith. First of all, when my daughter was born she was found to have Down's syndrome. This came as a most terrible shock and it numbed me for months. It had never occurred to me that I might have a handicapped child. I did want to write to you, I wanted to pour out all my distress in a way I couldn't do with Ann because obviously she needed my support. I don't think I did brilliantly on that score though. Then later on when I had come to terms with the situation and we had settled down to family life with a handicapped child, I started to think about you again. I had walked out of your life, out of *our* life, and how could it be helpful to you if I were to involve you, however peripherally, in what was happening in my subsequent one? I didn't regret what I had done, I wished it could have been achieved without giving you so much pain.'

'And your daughter, what has happened to her since her mother died?'

'As it turned out she is quite high grade and perfectly competent in a number of areas. She works in a garden centre and lives in her own apartment in a type of sheltered complex.'

'And you see her?'

'Of course. Once I had got over the initial shock, she became something very precious in my life, in both our lives. Within her parameters we communicate very well. I see her about once a week and I take her away on holiday. But, Faith dear, I don't want to talk about myself. When did this happen to you?'

'About a couple of years ago. I went for an early morning swim, you may remember those?'

'How could I forget. And what happened?'

'I clambered back on to the jetty and apparently collapsed. I don't remember. Luckily on that particular morning I wasn't the only swimmer. A tenant from the foreign-owned cottage was on the jetty. He was German, a doctor, and took the necessary action. I was in the clinic for about three weeks and then came back to the villa. Don't look so stricken. At least that wasn't your fault.'

'And everything else was. Have you ever found it in your heart to forgive me?'

'I'm not sure whether forgiveness comes into the equation. We human beings don't own one another. You never dissimulated, you had the courage of your convictions and I suppose that when we got together I took a calculated risk.'

'You're more generous than I deserve.'

'Deserve? What do any of us deserve? We weave our own cloth within the limitations of an elusive destiny. After all, your life after you left me wasn't exactly as you had expected or hoped.'

'No, it sure wasn't. But I would do the same again.'

'You deluged me with bitter unhappiness for quite a long period of time, but I too would do the same again. What we experienced in those years has never left me.'

'Nor me, and from time to time I return to it in my imagination, not in a spirit of sentimental nostalgia but because I draw from it strength to soldier on.'

They smile at each other, the crumpled middle-aged man and the stricken old woman.

'When did Ann die?'

'Two years ago when our daughter was rising seventeen. She was brave and fought it, and I believe and hope I helped her, but in the end it devoured her.'

'That's very sad. But at least you had a number of years together, which I hope were happy.'

'They were, and as you so rightly said what one has had can never be taken away.' Charles shifts in his chair and turns around to look through the French windows at the winter landscape.

'You must miss the sun,' he says, turning back to Faith. 'Tell me, what happened to the villa?'

'After I came back from the clinic, because I still had my marbles intact, I thought I might manage to stay on there with increased help from Maria. But my daughters made me see I was being unrealistic. So it was sold when

I came back to London. It was all done through agents so I know nothing about the people who bought it, nor do I want to.'

'It was a magical place. Do you remember the two cormorants in the summer months who used to sit very still on that low rock just above the waterline? And sometimes they used to swim with us?'

'Yes, I remember. They came back year after year and I liked to think of them as a faithful couple, though most likely they could have been different birds each year.'

'And you live with Hilary now?'

'Yes, Hilary and her companion, Winnie.'

'Oh I forgot.'

'What did you forget?'

'About Hilary...'

Faith experiences a small shiver of irritation. She feels tired, she has had enough.

'And America, how do you find living in the States?'

'It's my country now. I became an American citizen.'

'Oh. So it really was total amputation.'

'That's one way of looking at it. I prefer to see it as total integration, a complete bonding with the way of life I had so selfishly chosen.'

Faith glances hopefully towards the door. Surely Joss must soon be coming with that coffee. After which Charles would leave. Enough had been said and Faith has no interest in the everyday platitudes that remain. She knows that lost enchantment can never be recovered and that dead ash generates no flame. What had existed between herself and Charles is now internalised, and there is no external emotional space left for meaningful exchange.

Finally the door does open. Jocelyn comes through carrying a tray and as she tries unsuccessfully to close the door behind her with an elbow, Charles gets up and closes it for her.

Into the Rising Sun

I did enjoy my visit to Joss.

Faith keeps revolving this thought round and round in her mind like a mantra. But she knows that what she enjoyed most was getting back to Hilary and Winnie; to her versatile bed and her streamlined wheelchair, rather more than she enjoyed being away from them. How one's parameters shrink in handicapped old age, was her reflection on all this.

And then there was that meeting with Charles. It has receded, taken on a dreamlike quality, sunk into soft focus. Was it truly a healing act of reconciliation or simply a meaningless exchange between estranged persons? Faith likes to think it had some significance, if only because what she remembers of that period of her life remains bathed in sunlight. The pain and the unhappiness do also remain but as a cerebral memory only, no longer embedded in the fabric of her feelings.

This morning as usual, Faith is sitting in her wheelchair, facing the window. Susie is busy vacuuming down the corridor. Any moment now the door bell will ring – the ambulance arriving to take Faith to the day centre. A watery sunshine lights up the garden and the concrete path gives off a faint sparkle of melting frost. Faith peers out between the opened curtains, her failing eyes interpreting a different picture.

She feels tremendously tired despite a perfectly good night's sleep. Her right hand stretches out to switch off the radio on the table beside her. It is talk, talk, talk that is meaningless to her and she welcomes the ensuing silence.

An enormous wave of reluctance envelops her being. She does not want to go to the day centre. She has not wanted to go to the Centre for the whole of the past week. It was something she had looked forward to on her return to London – the day centre, seeing Sam again, talking to Sam. Maybe she would tell him about her meeting with Charles.

On her first morning back in London, Winnie had brought her the early cup of tea. Faith had pressed the familiar levers on her electronic bed (she hadn't forgotten how it worked, although she had called Winnie, Joss) and sat herself upright. Winnie had drawn back the curtains and kissed her fleetingly.

'It's nice to have you back. We missed you. I must fly, I'm late. Have a nice day at the Centre.'

She was gone before Faith could collect herself to reply. She sipped her tea contentedly and contemplated the day ahead. Hilary popped her head round the door to say good morning and goodbye, and shortly afterwards Susie brought in her breakfast tray.

She wanted to hear all about Faith's visit to Joss. Having never been out of London, Susie had difficulty in envisaging what 'the country' might be like. Faith described to her the big lawn with the tall oak at its centre and beyond in the distance the rolling, green Downs of Wiltshire. Had she seen her grandchildren? No, they were both away at university. And when she thought about the absence of her grandchildren she remembered there had been no dogs either. Households do change, children grow up, dogs die of old age or get run over, or worry sheep and have to be put down.

'No, Susie, neither grandchildren, nor dogs – it's a very quiet household now.'

She had arrived at the day centre and looked around in eager anticipation for Sam. He nearly always arrived before her but today there was no sign of him. She was left initially in the reception area by Bill and nobody had come as yet to take her elsewhere. She kept her eyes glued on the swing doors, expecting to see Sam in his chair pushed through at any moment. Still he did not come. She caught the attention of one of the carers who was passing through.

'Sam's late today, isn't he?'

The young man halted in his stride as if the sight of Faith reminded him of something he had to do. He came towards her and started to push her chair slowly towards the activity rooms.

'Sam won't be coming in any more. He had a heart attack over the weekend.'

He left her chair in the communal area and went off on his business. He was new on the job and Faith had never before had any dealings with him. As he passed out of sight Faith would have liked to have called him back, called him back and asked him to repeat what had seemed to her almost like a throw-away remark. She was not sure whether she had heard aright. She couldn't quite take in the import of what had been said. Perhaps Sam was only away temporarily, he would be coming back when he got better. Yes of course he would be coming back. An intermittent blip, these things happen in old age, one recovers.

Alice had come out of the art room and she came across to where Faith was sitting.

'Good morning. Did you enjoy your visit to your daughter?'

'Yes. Oh yes, I did. Very much.' But Faith did not want to linger on this subject, she hurried on to what was pressing on her mind. 'Alice, Sam isn't here today. That young man, you know, the new one, said he isn't very well.'

A look of concern had passed across Alice's face and she laid her hand lightly on Faith's shoulder.

'Faith, Sam isn't with us any more. He had a massive heart attack and went out like a light. For him, it was a good way to go.' As Faith made no reply, Alice continued. 'You were good friends you two, weren't you? You'll miss him, I'm sure. Would you like to come and do some painting to take your mind off things?' Alice began to push Faith's chair towards the art room.

All right. Why not paint? There would be no reading of the newspaper today, nor any of the days to follow.

Faith had found her good hand to be somewhat shaky as it held the brush and daubed paint on to the paper in desultory strokes and without any conscious design. *A good way to go.* Is there ever a *good* way to go? Faith's thoughts were random, and the line from Macbeth which so often in her life had come into her mind (especially when she found herself in uncongenial company) – *Stand not upon the order of your going, but go at once* – returned once again. But to whom she was addressing it she was not quite sure. Perhaps herself? She had made a last flourish on the paper and laid down her brush. Then she rested her hand on her solar plexus where the pain of loss was palpable. She pressed it gently but the pain would not go away. Then Alice had come round and stood by her chair.

'Oh Faith, it's the first abstract you've ever done. Quite impressive!'

That was over a week ago now. This morning, with the radio turned off, the flat is quiet apart from the hum of the vacuum cleaner. Faith slides into the doziness that so often overtakes her just before the ambulance arrives.

I can feel the gentle warmth of that early morning summer sun shedding its shaft of light along the smooth water. I have cast off my paralysis and now I am descending into the coolness of the sea. Not a ripple this morning as I strike out towards the risen sun. There is quietness all around. I am the only swimmer this morning and I feel as though I am enveloped in silk. I swim on, on and on and...

The buzz of the door bell reverberates shrilly. The vacuuming stops.

'The ambulance is here,' Susie announces, as she enters Faith's room – as she does every morning. She is about to propel Faith's chair towards the door when something alerts her. She bends forward to look more closely at Faith. A tiny gasp escapes through her fingers, raised to her lips in a sudden movement. She takes a step back, remains immobile for a second, then turns and runs from the room.

Hilary hands Charles the towel as he climbs out of the sea on to the jetty. He wraps it tightly round him and shakes the water out of his hair.

'Jesus it was cold! I don't think I've ever swum in March before.' He towels himself briskly and Hilary moves off down the jetty to join the others in front of the empty cottages. Winnie is standing between Maria (now hugely overweight) and Jocelyn who its chewing her lower lip in an effort not to cry. Winnie has an arm round each of them. Maria's daughters stand a little apart.

Charles wrestles himself into his clothes, which he had left in a heap on the parapet, and in a few minutes comes towards them pulling a thick pullover over his head. He had swum out on his back clutching the urn to his chest with one arm and using the other to guide him until he came to the green water over the patch of sand. Once there he trod water for as long as it took him to remove the lid from the urn and scatter Faith's ashes on the undulating sea. Then he dropped the urn and watched it sink to the sea bed.

It is a day of fitful sunshine emerging briefly in the gaps of grey cumulous cloud coursing across the sky, so that one moment it is chill and the next warm. The little group moves silently back to the cars on the path which rounds the whitewashed wall of the villa. Like the cottages it too gives off an air of winter evacuation – there is no one about.

Once back on the road they find their voices again. Maria leaves with her daughters, having invited the three women to a family meal the next day before they leave to return to London. Charles looks at his watch and says, 'I'll drop you off at the hotel and then I must sprint off to the airport to catch my flight.'

They get into his hired car and when they arrive at the hotel, Winnie bids him a brief but friendly goodbye and disappears inside. Charles has got out of the car and the three linger for a moment by the steps of the hotel. Hilary holds out her hand.

'Thank you, Charles, for coming all this long way. We really do appreciate it.'

'Thank you both for allowing me the privilege.' He gives Hilary a quick, diffident kiss and turns to Jocelyn. He offers her his hand.

'You haven't forgiven me, have you Joss?'

She takes his hand but looks at him unsmiling. 'No.'

Charles starts to get into the car but turns back.

'Oh I forgot, there's something I want you to have.' He fumbles in his trouser pocket and produces a folded piece of paper, somewhat creased and rather grubby. 'It's a poem Faith wrote years ago and I've kept it by me all this time. Now I think it belongs to you two.' He gives it to Hilary and then in moments all they see is the back of the car disappearing up the hill towards the main road.

Hilary walks up the steps into the hotel with her sister and accompanies her up to her room. Jocelyn sits down on the edge of her bed and Hilary sits down on the unoccupied one opposite.

'We did the right thing, Joss, even though you can't forgive him.'

'Oh I know we did. I hope perhaps Faith was with us in spirit. And all thanks to your inspiration and getting the plan in motion.'

'It didn't seem right somehow that her ashes should be scattered in some impersonal Garden of Remembrance. I felt it was fitting that she came back here to Pebble Cove where she spent so many happy years.'

'And so many unhappy ones.'

'Joss love, life is a lottery is it not? There are the big winners and the big losers and those of us who win a bit and lose a bit. We couldn't live Mum's life for her any more than she could live our lives for us.' Hilary gets up from the bed and gives her sister a gentle kiss on her forehead.

'And now I think we all need a drink. I'll go and find Winnie and see you in the bar.' She has just gone out of the door when Jocelyn calls after her, 'Hilary, what about the poem?' Hilary comes back.

201

'Yes, of course.' She takes the worn piece of paper out of her bag and hands it to Jocelyn. 'You read it.'

Jocelyn unfolds the paper and smooths it out on her lap.

Early Morning Swim

A grey silken sea.
Light of early morning
muted around the
fiery red ball of
the slowly rising sun.

Mirage like this ruddy globe
appears waterborne,
seems so close it might be
touched by the swimmer's hands
slicing the calm sea.

Then slowly floating upwards
the separation occurs.
It pales as it rises
from crimson through to pink, to white.
A miracle of change to see.

And now the lemon coloured sun
casts a white path aslant the water.
Across the bay the dawn-black promontory
beckons. Two cormorants accompany
the swimmer along the sunlit path.